THE MOOR IS DARK
BENEATH THE MOON

OTHER DAVEY BRYANT BOOKS BY DAVID WATMOUGH

Ashes for Easter (1972)
From a Cornish Landscape (1975)
Love and the Waiting Game (1975)
No More into the Garden (1978)
The Connecticut Countess (1984)
Fury (1984)
Vibrations in Time (1986)
The Year of Fears (1988)
Thy Mother's Glass (1992)
The Time of the Kingfishers (1994)
Hunting with Diana (1996)

ALSO BY DAVID WATMOUGH

A Church Renascent (1951)
Names for the Numbered Years (1967)
The Unlikely Pioneer (1985)
Vancouver Fiction (1985)

THE MOOR IS DARK BENEATH THE MOON

DAVID WATMOUGH

Away! the moor is dark beneath the moon.
—Percy Bysshe Shelley, "Stanzas—April 1814"

Porcepic Books
an imprint of

Beach Holme Publishing
Vancouver

This book is published by Beach Holme Publishing, 226–2040 West 12th Avenue, Vancouver, B.C. V6J 2G2. This is a Porcepic Book.

The publisher gratefully acknowledges the financial support of the Canada Council for the Arts and of the British Columbia Arts Council. The publisher also acknowledges the financial assistance received from the Government of Canada through the Book Publishing Industry Development Program (BPIDP) for its publishing activities.

The Canada Council   Le Conseil des Arts
for the Arts   du Canada

BRITISH
COLUMBIA
ARTS COUNCIL
Supported by the Province of British Columbia

Editor: Michael Carroll
Production and Design: Jen Hamilton
Cover Art: Copyright © Neil Robinson/Stone
Author Photograph: Edmond O'Brien

Printed and bound in Canada by Kromar Printing Ltd.

Epigraph from *The Romance of Tristan and Iseult*, as told by Joseph Bedier, translated by Hilaire Belloc, and completed by Paul Rosenfeld, copyright © 1973 by Random House, Inc. Published by Vintage Books, 1994.

National Library of Canada Cataloguing in Publication Data

Watmough, David, 1926-
  The moor is dark beneath the moon/David Watmough.

  "A porcepic book."
  ISBN 0-88878-434-1

  I. Title.
PS8595.A8M66 2002   C813'.54   C2002-911089-0
PR9199.3.W37M66 2002

For Floyd and fifty years

Dark was the night, and the news ran that Tristan and the Queen were held and that the King would kill them; and wealthy burgess, or common man, they wept and ran to the palace.

"Alas, well must we weep! Tristan, fearless baron, must you die by such shabby treachery? And you, loyal and honoured Queen, in what land was ever born a king's daughter so beautiful, so dear? Is this humped-back dwarf, the work of your auguries? May he never see the face of God who, having found you, does not drive his spear into your body!...But you, Tristan, you fought for us, the men of Cornwall..."

Night ended and the day drew near. Mark, before dawn, rode out to the place where he held pleas and judgement.... At the hour of Prime he had a ban cried through his land to gather the men of Cornwall; they came with a great noise and none but did weep saving only the dwarf of Tintagel.

—*The Romance of Tristan and Iseult*

ONE

"Are you going to her funeral?" Davey Bryant's lover asked. "I see here in the paper there are some incredible buys on the airlines. The old girl couldn't have died at a better time."

"I was thinking about it," Davey told Ken Bradley. "It's only two summers since we had her here, but it seems like yesterday. It was just six weeks and felt like forever. And to think, if she hadn't fallen ill it would have been the same all over again this year. Christ, what we've been spared! But if you say there's a ticket bargain to London, then I could take in her funeral and also get some new shirts for you at Gieves. I could see Cousin Alyson and her kids. Maybe take 'em to the London Zoo where they belong!"

Davey brightened then to the task of planning. "I could also bring back some things from Marks and Sparks. You're always complaining the stuff they sell here isn't the same, so we could stock up on the nonperishables. I could do all that before going down to Tintagel and burying her."

Ken leaned forward to ruffle his partner's silvering hair. "Yet another reason to thank Auntie for popping off now. You might bring back a local Cornish recipe for a genuine saffron loaf. I don't really like the one I've been using with the bread machine."

Davey attempted to smile seraphically. "That's because you don't really like saffron bread in the first place. You only bake it for me. I think you also believe I need a break and that's why you're encouraging me to go and see the old girl off after that excessively long and miserable life."

His partner of nearly forty years wagged a lawyer's finger in the style with which he'd so often addressed an accused in court. "You've got it all wrong, sweetheart. It's *I* who could do with you out of *my* hair for a few days. I want to go through all that crap in the cellar, give away stuff we'll never read again, and fling out some of the junk we've been accumulating for thirty-eight years. I can't do that with you around interrupting me and weeping sentimental tears." Ken carefully refolded the *Globe and Mail* and dropped it neatly on the stool by his armchair before turning to kiss the man who was almost identical in height as they were within months of the same age. He then left the spacious living room. Seconds later Davey heard the bathroom door slam.

The retired editor of a city newspaper, suddenly restless, turned and faced the plate-glass window. There were wraiths of mist around the base of the scattering of spruce and cedar that framed the view of the open Pacific halfway down the Sunshine Coast, some miles north of the Vancouver where he had previously worked.

Davey had been restless of late. Both of them had. Now they were both approaching seventy, and every day brought reminders that each wasn't quite as capable of coping so effectively with things as they had done a decade earlier. When he first stood and stared out that same window, most of the trees had been saplings, the lawn had been a field, and the landscaped garden was nonexistent. The human intrusion before their arrival had been hardly more than the occasional cutting of timber and sawing of logs.

He ruefully recalled that the distance to the open sand and sea had tended to be traversed by a limber and sprightly middle-aged gay couple—themselves when they first bought the silver grey Cape Cod house—rather than the slower-moving and now hoary-haired gents who walked with arthritic-paced steps and stuck prudently to the flagged path on the rare occasions they still boldly confronted the ocean at its very edge.

Davey thought of these things because of his Aunt Hannah. Compared with her, of course, they were still youthful! Over the past twenty months, since her steady decline from health and her finally quitting his late uncle's house and moving into the nursing home, she had attained her ninety-sixth birthday. And when she was being particularly gloomy in her scrawled letters—which was most of the time—he would write back and tell her they were both waiting to see her telegram from the queen when she made one hundred.

A deer sauntered across the lawn toward the clump of arbutus that screened them from the view of the Strait of Georgia. Davey moved closer to the window to watch. The deer was beautiful in its shyness and gliding motion yet appeared to lack any concern at the proximity of the weathered frame house at the edge of the forest. By its antlers, he could see it was a stag, and for some reason— maybe because it seemed more greyish than most of them around there—he thought it might be an old boy. But it wasn't limping and certainly held its head proudly high.

That brought him back to Aunt Hannah's last visit, and her incessant litany of aches and pains. It was a schedule relieved only by elaborate complaints about her neighbours in the village of Pentudy, whom she had learned to detest since the days of World War II when his Uncle Wesley had taken her home as a late-in-life bride with a face as plain as her smart London clothes were incongruous in that isolated Cornish village. Or so a judgemental twelve-year-old Davey had glumly observed of a newcomer—come, surely, to disturb their close-knit family life.

He didn't know how much Cornish memory lane he would have indulged in then and there, the deer now a white throat patch and a reddish buff coat creating an incredible camouflage from such a short distance, but at that moment Ken walked in to give Davey a playful punch in the back and ask if he wanted him to call a travel agent to see what airline had the better deal. Davey was instantly back in the immediate world before he could swivel round and answer yes. He was often embarrassed by his Cornish daydreams.

Ken's eyes brightened. He so loved it when Davey even verged on spontaneity. So much of the time his partner was distracted and either didn't answer Ken at all, or claimed the next day he'd never heard his query or comment. With an ardent mea culpa, Davey now flung himself into Ken's world of handling the challenges and chores of life as if for him, like the retired lawyer, it was also second nature.

Davey told him he'd go the very next day, after he called the Breakers (the old folks' home had notified him of his aunt's decease), suggested the following Saturday afternoon would be the earliest he could attend Hannah's obsequies, and asked them to duly inform the undertakers and anyone else they considered necessary.

He then so flung himself into the alien role of efficient being, *à la* Ken, that he was packed by noon and had reserved dinner for two at a small restaurant near Madeira Park, which Ken had recently discovered and in which he delighted. In fact, they both loved the restaurant's attempts to graft a French cuisine to the best of such local fare as the mushrooms and mussels, a special salad concocted from the establishment's own garden-grown vegetables and, of course, the abundant salmon and herring from the rivermouth waters on which La Périchole perched.

Before their sortie up the winding road to tackle gastronomic pleasantries and the kind of conversation they'd developed over the years for such sporadic *à deux* dinners in special places, Davey made a spate of phone calls to England and also, for the hell of it, to friends in both Paris and Vienna. He was even tempted to call George in Moscow, who was trying to construct a banking system along American lines. But Ken caught him searching for their friend's address and number and persuaded him that calling George merely to announce he couldn't see the man as he was only going to Cornwall to bury an ancient aunt wasn't only unnecessary but a gross waste of time and money. Common sense, as always, reigned with Ken.

The dinner was bliss. Well, almost so. Before the end the subject of Aunt Hannah arose again and, not for the first time, Ken mildly rebuked his partner for being so excessively harsh in judging her. Davey parried by asserting how incredibly she had nursed grievances over his conduct, way back as a child, when admittedly he had sometimes mocked her behind her back. Ken also insisted that the slapdash and self-indulgent Davey was far too exigent over someone who, after all, had been only a frail old lady without benefit of education and the kind of love they enjoyed with each other.

Davey saw there was a truth in the rebuke but that didn't necessarily improve his disposition. Typically they avoided any kind of outright rupture, but enough sense of discord adhered to them to assure an uncharacteristic silence on the drive home and through the familiar choreography leading to bed. They didn't forget to kiss each other good-night before plumping pillows and turning back to back, but this time there was no chirpy little comment about the congenial La Périchole and the pleasure of each other's company.

There, in the darkness, Davey shivered to the sense of that omission, but it hung as a disturbing presence about him the following morning when travelling at some thirty thousand feet and didn't dispel until the bustle of Heathrow and the subsequent challenge of London, Cousin Alyson, and her two ebullient offspring.

TWO

Alyson wasn't there when Davey arrived that afternoon at his cousin's house in Ladbroke Grove, but her two teenage children were only too much in evidence. He was disposed to ascribe his antipathy toward them to recent jet lag, but the truth was he had never cared much for either the few times he'd encountered them in the past. The conversation with them that now ensued while he impatiently awaited the return of their mother from shopping in the Portobello Road did nothing to increase his affection. To the contrary...

"It's Uncle Davey!" Hester said, her voice seeming flat with disappointment as she shouted the news back down the dark hallway to where her brother, Quentin, presumably lurked.

Davey managed a smile. "You can forget the *uncle* bit—like I said last time. Apart from it being inaccurate, you're both far too grown up now."

"I don't want to forget," she replied with a stubborn tilt of her witch's chin. "Where's Uncle Ken. Didn't he come, too?"

Once more Davey was relieved he'd rejected Alyson's invitation to stay with them and had booked into the Gresham as usual.

"Ken is busy. Besides, your Great-Aunt Hannah was often rather mean to him whenever she visited us. He hardly owes her! You're more family, come to that, but I gather from your mother that none of you intend to come down to Tintagel for the funeral." He sighed. "By the way, can I come in?"

Hester had the grace to nod, and he found himself following her clean-curved, fifteen-year-old ass in its too-tight, faded jeans as she squeezed more successfully than he past the two bicycles stacked against the walls. The mildly unpleasant smell was of fish.

"Quent is in the breakfast room where he's grooming his shitty dog. Mum said to make tea if you got here first, so we'll join him there."

"Neither of you at school then?" Davey asked, still addressing her posterior as he followed her to the deeper recesses of the gloomy house. "Taking time off for me? Should I be flattered?"

"It's a holiday, idiot! You forgotten all about English holidays out there?"

He strove for flippancy to match hers. "What's the point of trying to remember what you people seem to change every year? I thought these days you just went in for long weekends and, in any case, were always copying the Americans." Then quickly, in the hope it was before she could get her nasty little teeth into that, he followed up with: "So what are we celebrating? Martin Luther King Day?"

"Funeee! As a matter of fact, it's Michaelmas Day. Now that means it's the twenty-ninth of September, and I have a hunch, dear Uncle Davey, that you must think it's January 'cause, if I'm not mistaken, your murdered black leader is celebrated during that month."

He resisted the temptation to point out she was referring to the United States and not Canada. But he was also having difficulty in accepting the fact that he'd been completely unaware of what month it was, let alone the day. His immediate inclination was to dismiss the precision of dates as something his Ken always took care of. But the presence of this bumptious teenager and her seventeen-year-old brother whom he was about to confront made him uncomfortably conscious he was nearly fifty years their senior. Davey reflected dourly that only the old can be four months out in their diurnal reckoning. He grimaced to himself as he decided it would be prudent to let the matter of dates drop. So he said nothing as they entered the room where Quentin, stripped to the waist, was on his knees, carefully combing and occasionally trimming the ears of a handsome clumber spaniel. The boy didn't stop what he was doing but addressed the newcomer over his shoulder.

"Hello, Uncle Davey. Welcome to Ladbroke Grove. I'm sorry you caught me on Nigel's bath day, but I had booked today knowing I'd be home from school. Besides, Mumsie has been nagging about dog hair on her bloody furniture ever since last summer. Where's Ken? Shopping while you deal with the boring relatives?"

During their past two visits, both transatlantic visitors had nursed growing suspicions as to whether young Quentin would turn out gay or not. From vague remarks his mother had dropped, from the evidence of their own eyes and ears at some of his more outrageous comments, plus the occasional flip of a hip or limpness of wrist, there was gathering evidence to lead to the conclusion that either he was on the highway to queendom or that he must have prissy little fag friends at school or elsewhere whom he was seeking to emulate for some reason or other.

But for decades Ken and Davey had nursed a house rule between them: never suggest or even imply a homosexual likelihood about a member of each other's family or the sons of their friends to a third party. That is, unless their suspect freely provided such information about himself. But that had never happened.

Quentin, as Davey's youngest male second cousin, was the last in line to qualify as "family" who just might prove to be gay. But much as the two men covertly commented on his unkempt beauty, they would be the last to hint he might be more like themselves than the rest of his family. Accordingly, and perhaps with unwitting cruelty, they'd also be the last to proffer him any kind of germane advice.

In any case, Davey wasn't about to change tactics at this juncture as the boy sprawled lissome legs before him and shook those handsome curls away from the soft features of his still-puppyish face.

"Don't you think Nigel looks darling? All the bitches in the square think he's a doll, and so do some of the boys."

"I'll put the kettle on while you try to shock Uncle Davey," Hester told her brother. "You might also explain to him what the ridiculous Feast of St. Michael and All the Angels means and why it gives him the privilege of seeing his darling second cousins and not just their flustered mother."

In the event Quentin did no such thing. He did say it was a holiday at both St Hilda's School for Girls and his own Blesford Ride School, but for the most part he spoke of his adored spaniel, Nigel, and then of his plans to accompany three school pals the following summer to the south of France.

"Do you ever go to Cornwall these days?" Davey asked him when the kid had exhausted the lengthy description of his holiday plans.

"No. Why should I?"

Davey was taken aback. This kind of frankness wasn't the version he and Ken entertained. "Well, your mother…" he murmured. "I thought she was always going back to Falmouth."

"Only when her horrible parents were alive and blackmailed her. As soon as the Gramps were dead, she was finally free of all that Cornish balls—not to mention their revolting Methodism."

"So she sent us to posh schools—call that an improvement!" Hester was back with us, a tray of cups and saucers in her hand. "Personally, when I'm through at St. Hilda's, I shall be looking for a college—and a *country*, come to that—where God is seen as a piece of shit and religion generally as something that should've gone out with gaslight and horse-drawn buses."

"Hester's such a romantic," her brother commented from the floor. "At least my school doesn't flog God. We're more into dog than God at Blesford, aren't we, Nigel?"

"Milk and sugar—or are you gone all American?" Hester asked.

By now Davey was counting the seconds to his cousin's return from wherever the hell she'd gone. But he was still determined to remain temperate with these snotty "Brit-pricks," as he sometimes referred to them when discussing them with his partner.

"I'm surprised you should bother to ask yet again," he said. "For one thing you know I'm a *Canadian* and did *not* become a Yank. Your other mistake is more expected, as I get the impression you both have decided to stamp out any knowledge of your Cornish heritage. Such as *never* taking sugar in any beverage. Then isn't your generation desperately trying to be rootless, classless, and against national history so as to end up dutiful little Europeans? That would certainly account for the wholesale ignorance in your family's personal background."

"Oh, my God!" Quentin shrieked, abandoning his combing and rolling over a couple of times on the carpet. "We've got an Enoch Powell with us." He smirked. "An *E*noch not a *eu*nuch, that is."

Davey recalled the racist MP who had been a onetime British cabinet minister until fired for his attitude toward nonwhite immigrants. He wasn't flattered by the comparison. "At the right time and in the right place," he snarled, "I'll give you my liberal views on the brotherhood of man."

"On the sisterhood, too, I hope," Hester added pertly.

"And on the idiocies of linguistic feminism," he snapped in her direction. "In the meantime let's stick to the implications of the fact-starved view of history you both seem to exemplify. It is, of course, an early indication of the decline of civilization."

Sometimes Davey didn't like himself, particularly. This was one of them. Then he also resented the power of these youthful two to evoke the worst in him.

"Oh, come and sit down here, Hester, and listen to a lecture by our relation," Quentin invited. "Funny, though, I thought it was Uncle Ken, *the avenging attorney*—" he gave the title a broad American accent "—who might be more interested in that kind of thing while Uncle Davey just stuck to the daily dole of events from his newspaper."

"Let me pour his sugarless tea first," the girl suggested.

Before Davey could prepare himself for a further salvo a new voice entered what by now could reasonably be termed "the fray." It was Davey's plump and bustling Cousin Alyson who swayed in his direction, scattering multiple packages onto sofa and chairs while allowing a goodly portion of her wares to drop to the carpet.

"Now, Davey, dear," she chided, "I hope you haven't been quarrelling with the children. They were *so* looking forward to your arrival. Quentin was determined that Nigel look his most beautiful and Hester baked her biscuits—what do you call them, *cookies*, isn't it?— as she knows how much you love ginger, just as your mother did."

"How odd," he commented, "considering they were both quite ignorant of the fact I never take sugar in my tea."

"Uncle Davey says it's part of the ancient Cornish religion to hate sugar in tea," the pipsqueak sprawled on the carpet contributed. "He also says—"

"Uncle Davey can speak for himself, Quentin. Besides, I don't want a recap of *anyone's* conversation. I heard enough coming in. Davey, did you have a good flight?"

Davey sighed with the effort of reply. He was invariably depressed by his cousin's refusal, perhaps inability, to come to grips with anything. On the other hand, he reflected quickly, he could readily sympathize if she was merely striving to put distance between her and her mewling pups and their idiot blather.

"The flight was as unpleasant as I'd expected. No surprises. As long as the airlines remain determined to disturb sleep with their gross interruptions, long nocturnal flights will never be comfortable." He slumped back, satisfied that the observation, even if pompous, put space between himself and her offspring. However, he was forgetting their tenacity, not to say their impertinence!

"One mustn't forget, Mumsie, that Uncle Davey first went to America by sailing ship," Hester said. "It's hard to adjust when you get older. At least that's what Grandma was always saying when she moved in with us and started her nonstop complaining." She started to circulate both cups of poured tea and plates of gingersnaps as if she were presiding at some sedate garden party. She served Davey first.

He felt too fatigued—probably a further wave of jet lag added to his irritation—to deal with Hester's juvenile barbs. In fact, the self-image that clumped through his weary mind was one of those bulls of Pamplona—only one that was too long in the tooth to effectively vent its spleen against its puerile persecutors. In any case, Cousin Alyson, in her pacifically determined way, wasn't about to encourage feuding in her presence, although Davey thought she was motivated by a pathetic hunger to preserve family unity rather than defend her cousin from these vengeful little ageists.

So abandoning antagonisms, Davey let Alyson's words ooze over him, rather like the sun-warmed fringe of surf back home would sometimes trickle through his toes. Her kids, irritated, he suspected, by her gentle forbearance with the likes of her gay relative, began to disperse. First Quentin gathered up his canine toiletries and, with placid Nigel obediently at his heels, left for his "study" at the top of the house. Then Hester announced she wanted to see her favourite TV program, which was a series, she duly informed her second cousin, called *Tragedies of the Century from the* Titanic *to the* Hindenburg, and followed in her brother's wake.

A few seconds of silence ensued as Alyson moved to the chair her daughter had vacated and then initiated a discussion on their late Aunt Hannah, although that was only after a mild preliminary sparring over something Davey knew from long experience she'd bring up, even while praying she wouldn't.

"You'll stay with us, of course? The children have your room all prepared."

"Alyson, I didn't even know they'd be home. In any case, I booked in at the Gresham as usual. But I already told you that over the phone. Ken and I like the independence. We stayed there even when my parents were alive. It has nothing to do with affection or anything like that."

"I just thought...what with the funeral and our being her only living relatives." She sniffed, and for one awful moment he thought she was going to cry.

"You know very well, my dear, that if she hadn't been spending the summers with us in recent years I'd hardly be here myself. After all, she was only our aunt by marriage. By the way, I quite understand your not coming down there with me. It would be sheer sentimentality. And as far as those kids are concerned, rank hypocrisy!"

At least that got her off the staying-under-her-roof business, he exalted. Then, with a fresh burst of reproach emphasizing the worry lines of her face, she sought to excuse her absence from the funeral. "I would've gone, if you'd insisted, Davey. Whatever you say, my dear, she was still our Aunt Hannah. It's just that tomorrow happens to be my busiest. I could even have juggled my shut-ins with Mrs. Armstrong and taken hers next week. But tomorrow is Allen's birthday, and they phoned from St. Bride's to say he was having one of his better spells and might even recognize me if I were to bring him presents from his brother and sister and bake him a birthday cake." She paused. "He...he didn't last year." Then, as if to cheer them both up, she added, "At any rate, he isn't being violent this time."

As she talked about her schizophrenic son, Davey sat mute. He withheld eye contact, too. Allen was rarely mentioned. That was the final tragedy in an excessively scarred life that had included an early

and abrupt single parenthood from her husband's bloody expiry in
an auto accident in Normandy, and the subsequent presence of her
mother who had easily earned the title of monster during those
intolerable years the lady had stayed with Alyson and the three
young children in Notting Hill, after quitting Falmouth on the
wings of widowhood from a henpecked husband.

All of that was now stale if still depressing knowledge for Davey.
Sometimes he thought it should have linked them more firmly,
especially in a family where bonds were so close to being manacles.
But although Alyson was only ten years his junior—she'd married
late—her woes seemed to have forever placed her out front in the
family quest for inimitable martyr in the race for who bore the
heaviest crown. Indeed, by comparison, he knew they weren't only
leagues apart in that particular competition—his own life with Ken
appearing idyllic in comparison—but in so many other ways it
seemed they had inhabited differing worlds since adulthood separated them. And he knew that meant far more than geography.

His own degree of weaning from Cornwall had begun forty years
earlier and had surely been invigorated by a near-lifetime on another
continent that might as well have been another planet—and with a
mate whose roots were as firmly planted in California as his own
were in Cornwall. Yet, deep down, he was sorely aware he was still
bedevilled by his place of birth, a place she had managed to so
facilely shed for the lure of London and what he secretly called her
acquired English values. He was always aware that she persisted in
referring to the *county* of Cornwall, a wholly accurate designation,
while he clung to the misleading, because less specific, *duchy* of
Cornwall for its romantic Royalist and literary allusions.

He clenched hands until he felt nails digging into palms. Surely,
he told himself, it was significant that he alone was going to bury
Aunt Hannah on the morrow. Alyson and her offspring—whatever
the excuses—were *not*. That was all the accuracy of place he felt he
needed. He'd be there; they wouldn't.

But all that said, his irritation with her kids also notwithstanding, they still shared *something* he believed neither did with anyone else. It was an elusive thing, hard to name, hard to characterize. In Cornwall they would have been content to ascribe their bond to common bloodlines, but that was too facile for Davey. The son of the gene-conscious age, he was no longer satisfied with totem words for either the menace and tyranny or the shared joys and insights from their inherited genetic bank.

They shared a volatile sense of childhood, liking the same relatives and equally scorning others. Another thing he relished was their ability to trust each other to a profound degree.

He knew a peace in her company that wasn't only at violent odds with the feelings her children set up in him, but which he knew she reciprocated. If only she didn't sometimes bore him… But where was perfection? he ruefully asked himself, concluding his little meditation.

In spite of poor Alyson's endless attempts to calm the choppy waters that Quentin and Hester perversely animated, Davey believed she identified basically with him, her only cousin, and that this went beyond the claims and instincts of her own offspring. The frequent signs that the ever-potential rift between her children and himself was painfully troubling to her he took as evidence of what they shared from their own childhood past. Put simply, he silently argued, Alyson and he loved each other in a very Cornish family manner. And like all true human riches, such love was effortless— unimpeded by all the separations and vastly different attitudes to overcoming the hurdles and ambushes of the days.

Why, then, all this being true, he asked himself, did they fret and peeve as they sat there that late-September afternoon, discussing Aunt Hannah and what had set her apart from the Bryant clan?

If it wasn't her children, then surely it was what they stood for: that ineluctable Englishness they had absorbed and what, in a narrower sense, they had inherited as teenage Londoners in today's world. Some historical umbilical cord had been severed and their mother was powerless to mend it. The fluke of gayness, the chance of geography, had removed him, only to confirm him, paradoxically, in that Cornish ancestry they had repudiated and duly lost.

Life, the aggressive *present*, had also persuaded Alyson that her Celtic past was moribund and that survival for her from the wounds that littered and weighted her past meant a total grasping of the world she now inhabited and caring not one whit for the one she had left: that snug, crescent of a harbour and scattering of alien palms along the Falmouth front that stretched beyond the bay and lipped the English Channel's mouth.

"You say you don't want to reconsider staying here with us? That would give you and me, Davey, one of the few times we ever get to talk anymore. Surely we owe that to each other, now that no one else is left."

"Alyson, we are talking now."

"You do understand about Allen, dear? Why his improved condition makes it impossible for me to accompany you?"

"Of course I do! Quentin and Hester are something else, though. Not that for one moment I need them as companions."

She shrugged plump and rounded shoulders. "They are free agents, aren't they? I can't *force* them. They expressed no interest— any more she in them. Then they hardly knew her, did they? Oh, dear! Why does everything end up in questions?"

"The simple truth of the matter, Alyson, is the fact she was the end of something. And that something is all tied up with just you and me. We're the end of the Bryant line. We're looking at the bare bones, the carcass of what we so long took for granted as the family."

"You did maybe as a single man. But not my children, not their generation. They've been reared so differently. Their values… Well, Davey, surely the whole world has changed."

"We will still never understand those changes unless and until we've all said our goodbyes to what precipitated them. Even your kids came out of something, not just a London limbo." He could see by the obstinacy giving faint contour to her fleshy features that she was unconvinced. "Anyway, let's drop it. I'd rather stick with what we have in common than waste time on what pushes us apart. Alyson and Davey…all that's left."

She wiggled her ample bottom uncomfortably in the armchair as always, resisting bleakness, fighting harsher realities, realizing if she had capitulated to that in the past it would have broken her. "I suppose in the end, Davey, I'm just a silly old mother. That's what everything comes back to in the end. I can't help it. *Someone* has to think of the shopping."

He stared at her. How he wanted to admire her, knowing her virtues, her powers of self-sacrifice that he believed far beyond him. But he couldn't help an irritation welling over her exaggerated mother bit, of her wasting her substance over two kids who already inhabited another universe from the one she understood. Teenagers who were already set to go their own way, leaving her by the way-side. He conceded then and there that he was probably jealous of them. In any event, he knew he had no right to upset her by scoffing at her maternity, however simplistic it sounded. If he even hinted at all that, he knew she would only end up rounding on him as a child-less bachelor without either the instincts or experience to understand.

"Here's to motherhood, old girl," he said instead, holding up an imaginary glass in toast to her.

"Here's to us both, Davey," she responded similarly.

As shortly after that as he could, again carefully avoiding hurting her feelings, he guiltily made his departure, promising her with excessive emphasis that he would call her from their shared birthplace.

On the train the next morning, circuitously heading to Tintagel via Okehampton, it occurred to him that this was the second voyage since leaving home that he was encompassed with a sense of guilt that wouldn't go away: first, after leaving Ken under less than warm circumstances, and now because of Alyson whom he'd somehow failed to comfort. He emerged from his compartment on the last train leg of the journey in a black depression as he sought to hire a car for the final part of the exhausting trip.

THREE

Davey looked about him over the rows of pitch-pine pews in the squat slate chapel perched on the heathered cliff top. There were five people scattered about the drafty space. For a deceased without immediate family, he surmised, it was the local custom for the coffin to remain in the funeral home until after the service when a hearse would drive it to a churchyard—in this case Pentudy's—and the undertakers would provide professional bearers before burial. He hadn't volunteered for the task.

The others were strangers to him. Then Hannah had no relations in Cornwall and only five—if one included Alyson's three children— in that larger world beyond the windblown headland stubbornly confronting the uninterrupted Atlantic.

In the front row of the sea of empty pews huddled a close-sitting couple. They both looked middle-aged and each wore navy blue belted raincoats. The woman's head was covered in a gaudy red-and-white kerchief, while her companion, at a dig from her, suddenly pulled off a Donegal tweed hat and placed it on the pew beside him. The action revealed a grizzled head of close-cropped hair. They were wearing rubber boots that evoked the incessant rain prevailing outside. There was something vaguely familiar about the two to the Canadian, and he wondered if, in spite of his conviction that only he and Alyson's family were left, they might be relatives he'd utterly forgotten. They were both *very* short, even shorter than he who was only five foot six, and as he eyed them he strove to recall if there had been others in the family who, at a pinch, might have been described as dwarfs. The reflection brought no immediate results, so he turned his attention elsewhere.

Facing the miniscule congregation was their opposite in height—a tall, dank man in a dark brown corduroy suit who announced in a sepulchral voice that he was the local lay preacher on the North Cornwall Methodist Circuit. Davey guessed he might also be the local undertaker. His ashen skin certainly looked as if he'd spent most of his days burying the dead under sunless skies and in driving rain.

Behind and above the preacher's bobbing, balding head with its few flat strands of carefully arranged hair was a sign curving over the generous pulpit space he occupied. It read COD IS LOVE. Davey took a moment or two to realize that the bar of the *G* had fallen off or worn away. He sniffed his satisfaction. His sense of geography evidently hadn't let him down. He recalled that the isolated spot where the chapel was defiantly situated was only a mile or so south of the fishing village of Poltiddy, itself south of Tintagel, where any species of fish, along with the local mackerel, lobster, and crab, provided the fishermen contingent of the local inhabitants with a precarious living. COD IS LOVE seemed more germane there as a source to pray to than obeisance to some remote and distinctly unfishy deity.

The service struck the deceased's nephew as indecently short. He was subconsciously expecting, if not a full-blooded requiem, at least something that bespoke *departure*. Along the lines, say, of "Farewell, Thou Christian Soul." In his mind there were vague echoes of Edward Elgar's stately *Dream of Gerontius*, a composition, based on Cardinal Newman's poem, of which he and Ken were extremely fond. Instead the chapel was filled with the staccato squawks from a dumpy harmonium now pressed into service by a white-haired woman in mackintosh to match, who hunched over her modest instrument in that Spartan Methodist tabernacle as if she were Wanda Landowska at the harpsichord.

But there now reluctantly stirred in Davey a bundle of memories that had been quiescent, if not suppressed, since he'd first headed for North America in the company of Ken. He was remembering the pull from the distaff side of his family of that Primitive Methodist Connection that had determined his youthful attendance in Trelinney Chapel for Sunday Morning Service and Sunday School.

There now vividly returned divers recollections of the battery of onerous Sunday sorties to chapel that had been dovetailed into the equal Sabbath obligations of Anglican Mass and Evensong. As the tiny congregation bawled—with little seeming relevance to the circumstances of Great-Aunt Hannah (or, indeed, the weather)—the sprightly chorus of "Jesus, wants me for a sunbeam," Davey's thoughts turned to an onerous past; to those infinitely dull annual Sunday School outings to the surf (forbidden to enter) and sand (only the top part which the tide rarely washed) of Polzeath Beach instead of the church's more exciting expeditions to more distant places such as St. Ives, Penzance, or Land's End.

From "Sunbeams" the creaky harmonium led the congregation to the hymn "All Glory, Lord, and Honour," after which the exhausted throats were reminded by the preacher that "Methody was born in song." They were then asked to inform their Wesleyan God just how happy they all were to have known his saint, Hannah Bryant, who had valiantly darkened the doors of Cornish Bethels since her remote childhood. This was a detail that was news to

Davey who had vaguely been under the impression that her "remote childhood" had been lived in London.

Then it was soon evident from the preacher's florid oratory that he knew next to nothing about Mrs. Hannah Bryant, other than that she had passed the last few months in an old folks' home called the Breakers where she'd also expired. He referred to her "valiant battle"—*valiant* was a favourite word with him—with cancer and, somewhat incongruously, that she was an exceptionally well-travelled woman. His balding head then turned in Davey's direction as he obliquely added that evidences of that were there in the chapel with them that very afternoon.

The object of the reference quickly bowed his head, not through modesty but in a stubborn determination not to make eye contact with someone who was patently grasping at straws. Such determination was to prove in vain. The preacher was at Davey's side before he could reach the pitch-pine doors. The man offered him every cliché of condolence in the book before introducing him to the rain-coated couple as "Hannah's grandson." The Canadian wouldn't even have bothered to correct the preacher had not the information invoked immediate and unmitigated looks of hostility from the two dwarfs. Davey was forced to confront them whether he liked it or not. They were both even shorter than he'd first thought. With wrinkled, wind-tanned flesh and dark, furtive eyes, they might also have been brother and sister.

At the threshold to the moan of the wind and the hiss of rain the woman spoke up. "Us didn' know as how Hannah had a grandson. Ask me husband. Never spoke of 'un, did her, Len?"

By now Davey knew that whatever else had gone, the Cornish dialect hadn't died out in North Cornwall. "Len" confirmed it. "Oi bide there were none but a nephew and he lived a brave way away. Foreign parts, Oi reckon. By the way, we'm Len and Hilda Verran."

Davey didn't extend his hand.

The object of their attention addressed them in a slightly

Southern accent, filched from excessive observances of Vivien Leigh in *Gone with the Wind*. "You are addressin' the very same! Across the water from where we stand," Davey added, pointing toward Newfoundland. "I come from afar, ma'am, but I represent her other four kin—all of them residents of this island if not exactly in Cornwall but none of whom, from mental distress or other pre-occupations, are able to be here with us this afternoon."

Mrs. Verran attempted a smile. "We was her closest friends, we was, as well as her *Tintagel cousins*. She did mention of 'ee, didn' her, Len? Full of kind words for 'ee, she was. Her was allus speaking of your *friend* and that lovely house you two do have. Down by the Pacific Ocean, Oi think her did say?"

"Was *allus* saying," her diminutive husband interrupted. "Talked of little else when her moind was working. Not that that were too often. Till we persuaded her to go into the Home we had to spoon-feed her, you. And bravun more'n that, Oi don' moind a-telling of 'ee. If 'twasn' for Hilda here, Hannah Bryant would have been in some messy state, you. Hilda made her loife worth living these past years. Whole village will tell 'ee that. Little to show for it, though there's some will tell 'ee otherwise. Spiteful bastards!"

"Come now, Len, no need for bad language," his spouse reprimanded, offering Davey such a sickly leer that he could have upchucked.

By this time Hannah's nephew also gathered the Verrans were fluent liars. The old girl would never have mentioned Ken and himself in the same breath, let alone their sharing a house. His betting was they'd been through her correspondence like an avid brace of ferrets. More, he knew of no *Tintagel cousins*, though the idea brought with it the earlier vague notion that they looked somehow familiar. Not that at that point he sought further elucidation.

Davey's palms sweated with discomfort. These two unwholesome relics of Aunt Hannah's final phase of life, he told himself, reeked of cupidity. A brace of money-grubbers, they obviously

scented potential recompense from him. Perhaps they'd also discovered the fact that his aunt had died skint, that she didn't even
own Lanoe, the house she'd lived in, as that had reverted to Alyson
and him when Hannah's sister-in-law, their Aunt Nora, had died

As Davey stared down at the Verrans, he imagined how, as arduous
little maggots, they must have wriggled their way into his aunt's
trust as her pain-wracked body moved steadily toward its final state
of collapse. Whether they had or not, peasant cunning determined
that he now be regarded as a potential stone to be turned carefully
over lest there be further trove from an unwanted link to Hannah
they hadn't contemplated, turning up now at her funeral.

He told himself he hated them for that—detested them for
thinking he was going to be an easy make. Then he drew back.
Where, he thought, suddenly bewildered, was his mind taking him?
A kind of contempt for their mercenary attitudes over his aunt was
one thing, but he was experiencing visceral feelings that went far
beyond that. Whence came this vigorous loathing of an odd little
couple who had been utter strangers until minutes earlier?

He decided to blame it on the recently experienced funeral
service. It had jabbed strange questions and released doubts in him
that had lain dormant for decades. In their thick Cornish accents
this couple merely confirmed with a vengeance that he was back in
his ancestral lands. It had all happened too quickly, with not enough
space between the jerky train and the thick fog of his depression
and the driving up to the chapel on the blustery headland and being
pitchforked back into the bluff and energetic Methodism that had
pursued him in his childhood.

He sought now as alternative to play little games with the
Verrans—wild fancies that would curb his sudden animosity and
hopefully distance himself from the pair. "Aunt Hannah was so
modest," he began. "She never wanted to talk about all that coal-mine
money Uncle Petherick left her after he immigrated to Pittsburgh.
And I guess she told you more, as her best friends, than she ever

told me about the Texas property of old Petherick's daughter, Loveday, and the oil well she inherited from her second husband?"

Stroking a beardless chin, Davey looked out of the tall doors at the leaden sea. "Funny," he mused, "I guess most of the fortune she was left came from the United States rather than Canada where all she got was the Alberta ranch. I don't expect she left too much over here, did she? Then the house was never exclusively hers, of course. When her dear sister-in-law died, Cousin Alyson and I divvied up the proceeds of Lanoe House with her and let her stay there rent-free while she lived. Not that she needed anything like that with all the American loot. Then who am I telling? You got all the information when the will was read, of course."

Hilda Verran could contain herself no longer. She let out a hiss of air surprisingly loud for one of her stature. *What* will? We b'aint heard of no will! There bin no will read, has there, Len? Jest a penny or two lying about the house, and bits o' furniture that was hardly more'n matchsticks. Curtains was in rags from the first day Oi see'd 'em!"

Her husband glanced up at Davey's face and probably saw the smirk lurking there. He grabbed at her sleeve. "There were a derelict old Austin out back. No more'n a pile of junk that was! Least it help pay getting her into the Breakers. Otherwise she'd have been on the parish."

Davey thought the man was expecting his sympathy, when he felt much closer to erupting in laughter. Fortunately for the Verrans that was the moment the organist and preacher elected to depart. There was a smile for Davey from the uncertain musician, who then accorded the preacher a grudging nod as the tall figure, now wrapped in a bright yellow oilskin, bolted the doors of the chapel behind all five of them. He gave his erstwhile congregation a deep-throated adieu before stepping toward his muddy vehicle and, Davey hazarded, another funeral on his scattered circuit of rural Primitive Wesleyan chapels along the North Cornwall coast. The lady left on a bicycle.

The three remaining regarded one another. In accordance with his earlier resolution Davey smiled at them both as two upturned faces, their expressions flitting from anxiety through skepticism to outright hostility with the regularity of traffic lights.

Their disconcerted looks were matched with an excited, high-pitched babble. Mr. Verran was the loudest, his spouse the more voluble, but it still remained a hysterical chorus from the little couple. "Will? Oh, no, sir! No bloody will!"

"Her never, ever mentioned that money, did her, Len? Money in *America*? Money in *H'Alberta*? Never! Never! Be sure on that, maister. Her allus claimed to be as a church mouse. What a hussy! And her hiding a bloody fortune?"

That was the first expletive Davey had heard fall from the lady's lips.

"Her left nothing in Lanoe that a Gypo would drop by for!" Len chimed in. "Oi can tell on 'ee that! Cryin' poor mouth, with all that tucked away over there! Regular miser, then, was our Hannah Bryant! Devious biddy!"

"Miser and hypocrite! A lettin' of us *slave* over her all them years! And to think her could've had a regular bunch of servants awaitin' on her every wish and whim!" Hilda paused for a breath.

Davey shifted his weight onto the other leg. Their frantic litany was beginning to bore him. It was then he came to a decision that was to have far-reaching implications, far more than he could have ever anticipated. Besides, his adopted playfulness was shot with cunning. He suddenly saw a way of temporarily ridding himself of these tiresome two who claimed to be cousins and at the same time extending their punishment for their greedy insinuation into old Hannah's life.

"Maybe she did make a will," he began, "and then hid it some-where in the house. Auntie was so suspicious about a lot of things." A fresh inspiration sustained his invention. "Of course, it would be made out to you people. There was really no one else, you see. She told Cousin Alyson and me that the proceeds from the house would be all we'd ever get. She might have mentioned the North Cornwall Hunt or some dogs' home in Newquay as beneficiaries, but that would have been before you guys moved in. I mean, before she had your help and loving care."

They exchanged quick glances. Davey felt he could feel them secretly slobber over the references to both fox hunt and dogs' home. He felt sure they would be aware of the two incidents in his aunt's life of which she moaned endlessly. One involved the littering of her land by defecating foxhounds, the other her spirited defence of her treacherous dog who apparently had turned on her, disfiguring her face and nearly biting her to death.

The Verrans couldn't contain themselves. "Oh, her would've had no truck with the loikes of they!" Hilda shouted.

"Sued the master of hounds over the North Cornwall and the shit its dogs dropped all over her lawn!" her husband exclaimed. And, as further elaboration: "And Oi reckon she were moinded to have all bloody dogs outlawed after she were savaged by her own. No, my handsome, there'd be no money going to them outfits. Not bloody likely!"

"More than that Oi reckon we got no more to say." Whether Hilda was merely upset by her husband's language or whether she was fearful of one of them saying too much—now that the prospects of personal enrichment had become so much closer— Davey was unsure, but he opted for the latter. Articulation was always risky where he and they came from: he recalled afresh how deep went Cornish superstition.

"I have an idea," he volunteered. "Why don't we all slip over to Lanoe and see what we can find?" Then, lest they were reluctant to accompany him, he added, "There's a problem of time, you see. I mean, if in Canada and the U.S. they don't hear of a will, they might simply regard her as intestate and hand over all her assets to the state."

Even as he said it, Davey thought his spur-of-the-moment argument crass, but he realized at that juncture he was relying not so much on his powers of persuasion as on the blindness of the greedy. He blew the gods a kiss as the Verrans scrambled over each other verbally to shout their instant agreement with his cockeyed proposal.

In a matter of minutes both their ancient Morris Mini van and his rented Rover were revving loudly against the cry of the wind. As the two vehicles headed south on reaching the coastal highway, the dwarfs quickly passed him and he lost sight of them. That didn't faze him, though. He was looking forward to driving at a leisurely pace through the network of narrow, leafy lanes on leaving the main road and heading for Pentudy with its fondly remembered Celtic cross dominating the village green. It was at least twenty years since he'd seen the village where "Lanoe" was his family's "dower house" and where each Bryant generation had gone in succession from the neighbouring parish where the eldest sons had always farmed so that the two village churches shared in the family christenings, marriages, and occasional burials over at least three centuries.

But during that return to the past Davey was to learn that the "new Cornwall" he was about to experience, albeit briefly, was savagely different from the one he'd left behind. Of course, he was about to change his mind concerning a whole lot of things, not least about his relatives dead and alive, his lifetime companion back in British Columbia, and finally himself.

FOUR

ornwall had always been a place for Davey Bryant that shored up romantic and conservative beliefs. Everything about it served not only a faith in the past but proclaimed that past would endure. The very granite and serpentine from which the peninsula had been honed by millennia of grinding seas affirmed the stubbornly permanent finger poking out from western Europe. So did the unceasing surf that pounded it. Likewise the wind-scoured skies that turned silver mist into azure in one powerful breath. Raven-haunted moors would never be fields, Dozmary Pool would never dry up, and the scream of gulls and swoop of martins would festoon the cliffs facing fabled Lyonnesse forever.

All these images and convictions had entered Davey's soul, from its first beat in that farmhouse reached only by unsurfaced, fern-bordered lanes and where drinking water, sweet with purity, was carried by sturdy men and women in giant buckets from the moss-screened well at the foot of the elm-clad hill where badgers lived in centuries-old setts.

And if the time warp wasn't enough, there was also the isolation: a mile's walk between heather and fern to the neighbouring farm whose tenants might not be seen for a month and whose presence might only be proclaimed by Mrs. Hoskyn's calling to her upfield calves or the sound of her husband's milk pails as he strode at sunrise to the cowshed and the clanging of their handles as he dropped them under an udder—weirdly muffled on morning mist—came to him over the boulder- and bracken-strewn valley. Seven miles away to Wadebridge, just under that to Camelford. But where were you when you reached such places?

Davey knew early in life that he lived some two hundred and fifty miles from London and eight hundred miles or so would get him near John o' Groat's, the northernmost tip of the British Isles, but all that was nothing to a boy accustomed to standing on Tregardock Cliffs and staring across toward North America over two thousand seven hundred miles westward and recalling how many of his relatives had sailed over there in the past hundred years or so. More Cornish folk, proportionately, than had fled the famine in Ireland.

All these verities that made pygmies of time… Then there were the domestic intimacies that had snared him yet more firmly: the great brass bed of his birth glowing dim in the flickering oil-lamp light, where his mother had groped and gripped at the bedclothes in the bridal bedroom of ancient Polengarrow, where red Virginia creeper grew over slate sidings screening mother and son from the teeming life of the surrounding farm.

He remembered other things: the burr of soft Cornish voices always in the ears; the smell of saffron-laden kitchens never far from the nostrils; the ubiquitous slate stiles in the hedges for pedestrian shortcuts along paths beaten by carless country folk walking from village to village, town to town; the huddled county town of Bodmin, full of friendly fish-and-chip shops but with grim, high walls for both a prison and a lunatic asylum through whose giant gates the mentally stricken would shuffle at full moon after having trudged down so many paths bordering fields and clambering over so many stiles, from white cob cottages often thirty or forty miles distant.

But now this kaleidoscope of recollections began to wobble. Instead of footpaths he was aware of so many gas stations festering the highway. Rows of new concrete-faced houses littered the outskirts of Delabole and Camelford as they had, indeed, of the Tintagel where he'd begun his journey in the wake of the Verrans.

Pylons suspending high-tension cables sprawled across fields double the size of those he'd left behind as their hedgerows had been bulldozed and where he now saw tractors at work rather than horses. Every now and then there were giant billboards that made him grind his teeth, and the far-off China clay pits around St. Austell seemed to have tripled in number whenever they hove in to view. Nor was he prompted to forget that he had had to rent his car in remote Okehampton in Devon, since no trains any longer served his part of Cornwall.

Yet all these visual aggressions and unnerving changes were fleeting and only half-caught as the curving highway seethed with traffic and he had to concentrate hard on both steering wheel and brakes.

By the time he turned off the A-39 and entered the slower pace and elm-tree cool of the winding lanes, he experienced the sudden rusticity as a needed benison that would prevent his skull from cracking. When he eventually reached the final hill outside and overlooking the village of Pentudy, he felt finally cleansed of the highway dreck, and his spirits rose in response to the abrupt change of weather so Cornish in its capriciousness. And he welcomed a sun-shot sky with the coastal wind now given way to a gentle breeze that carried the burnt scents of autumn and the murmur of bees. Then his sight concentrated on the starkly familiar edifice of Aunt Hannah's Lanoe House with its lime wash differentiating it from its whitewashed neighbours. Parked immediately in front of it was the

Verrans' Morris. He smiled, bemused by the fact that even the ridiculously battered and muddied old minivan was a relief after the hourlong preview of contemporary Cornwall in its festoon of high wires, untidy car cemeteries, and blatant roadside advertising—a place obeisant to tourism and its ugly adjuncts in which he was already convinced he had no proper place.

But if Davey was now the interloper—certainly in the eyes of the Verrans and most likely in the minds of the villagers of Pentudy who "knew not Joseph," as his biblically versed grandmother would have surely quoted—he felt another conviction perversely but determinedly growing in him. He wasn't just there to bury an old and unhappy woman who had lived for decades at odds with her neighbours, not even to safeguard her meagre chattels from these Tintagel interlopers, but now in new and startling resolve not to leave until fully possessed of that life in Pentudy that had become progressively beleaguered after the early death of her husband, also a Joseph, the beloved younger brother of Davey's patriarchal farmer father, Wesley.

He drove by the granite Norman church whose presence dominated the western entrance to the village, past the smithy, whose bellows and anvil could be seen from the open road, past the ugly house that now belonged to only him and Alyson—whatever the Verrans believed—and at which site, until short minutes ago, he had contemplated pulling up and joining them for the fictitious search for the will, and parked instead in the courtyard of the Cornish Arms, the only hostelry in the remote moorland village.

Switching off the ignition, he raced through a "Hail Mary," subconsciously invoking a dusty religious past and perhaps preparing himself to enter a territory and a time in which the darker things pertaining to his aunt in that isolated life would become intelligibly clear and which he could one day explain to his Cousin Alyson and the two doubters under her roof. And hopefully, as postscript, he could deal with the Tintagel pygmies who seemed bent on feeding off the detritus of her death.

An earlier phone call on arrival in Tintagel before the funeral service had secured his reservation, and in the meantime the current if
temporary inhabitants of Lanoe were the immediate challenge. He
decided to check into his booked room, after the encounter with
them at Lanoe.

In spite of himself, as he crossed the threshold of Aunt Hannah's
domain, the memories gusted. Nearing the steep, plum-carpeted
stairs that faced the front door, he again knew the claustrophobia in
their narrow steepness between bare distempered walls that
formed grotesque maps of dried damp: an immediate reminder for a
small boy of threatening goblins and nasty gnomes as he had pushed
bare knees in a frantic effort to climb them as fast as his thin legs
would allow to reach the cold little room his two aunts called "his"
whenever he stayed there and they decreed it was time for bed.

The cold had been one thing, the darkness another. "You're far
too old for a hot-water bottle," sallow Aunt Nora, with her distinct
moustache, had told him dismissively in answer to one piped question,
followed swiftly by "Who needs a nightlight when you've Jesus nailed
above you on the wall, you faithless boy!" And when he persisted in
sharing the thought with her that in the unholy dark Jesus would be
no good to him, followed by the observation that he knew where
you could buy phosphorescent crucifixes that would glow Christ's
goodness and keep the demons away, she slapped his bare arm and
accused him of blasphemy.

Scared of her, yet still propelled to ask her for heat and light in his
weekend bedroom at Lanoe House, she would invariably threaten
to leave him behind when she attended the seven o'clock Mass on
Sunday mornings. That was something he couldn't bear to contem-
plate. He never wanted to be left alone with silent Uncle Joseph
who rarely left his study except to rant at anyone's God as all deities
had been absent from the mud of Flanders when and where he'd
most needed them or, even worse, with moist-lipped Aunt Hannah

who was always wanting to smother him with kisses and tell him that he was the little boy she'd always wanted to have.

He could never decide which was worse—all that luvvy stuff or tall Aunt Nora, who not only hated warmth and light but was always silent on the way to church, while yanking painfully at his arm to make him keep up with the enormous strides of her hairy legs (he'd glimpsed her one Saturday afternoon in the bath). They were the only two occupants to flee the numbing cold of Lanoe on a Sabbath dawn, though obviously that wasn't something she had in mind. Perhaps she was trying to make up for naughty Uncle Joseph who, she said, had become a pagan because of his dreadful experiences before coming home from the Great War. Listening to Aunt Nora as a child, Davey got the impression that her beloved brother's loss of faith was far worse than all the wheezing and coughing he did even before taking out his leather tobacco pouch and rolling and smoking his own cigarettes.

With Aunt Hannah it was different. Her sister-in-law told him the reason she wasn't at early Mass was because she was a lazy Methodist and everyone knew *they* only got up early when there was a chance to make money.

After Davey and his aunt got inside St. Brychan's, the name of the patron saint of Pentudy Church—the two of them were always early— they would be subsequently joined by a scattering of worshippers: ghosts among the deep shadows beyond the array of flickering candles on the votive stand at the entrance to the Lady Chapel where the early Masses were always said.

When she wasn't complaining to him about his filthy boyish habits, Aunt Nora seemed to enjoy shocking him. Standing there at the foot of the stairs, some sixty years later, he still recalled her saying to him, "Of course, I prefer the First Mass of the day. There are no damn people you have to talk to before or after. And they don't want to have some stupid chat with you, which is even better!"

As he heard the Verrans skittering toward him from the direction of the kitchen at the back of the house, he conceded, in spite of himself, just how much they belonged. It was because they blended so congruously into that remote ancestral world he kept recalling: of a sadly dehydrated marriage between his uncle and aunt, of the ever-present animosity between childless Aunt Hannah and her stubborn spinster of a sister-in-law, and of their mutual dislike that, even in his child eyes, had seemed to embrace them like the contracting convulsions of a hungry python. That strangling serpent that had entwined them only increased its pressure with the departure of their *umpire*—the sole man of the house—who finally succumbed in his fiftieth year to the mustard gas that had lurked in his lungs since he encountered it, unsuspectingly, on the battlefields of France.

Davey had never really known his uncle, but now he wondered what the man would have made of these two upstarts who approached him, fiddling with anxiety and popping endless questions about where they should start the hunt and who should accompany whom. He guessed they had no intention of leaving him on his own in what they constantly referred to as their home, so he suggested they all simultaneously and methodically search each nook and cranny however crowded they were.

What was quite obvious was that by then the Verrans knew every room as intimately as his Aunt Hannah had. As he pretended, sometimes with ludicrously exaggerated gestures to search for the imaginary will, he managed also to draw a few squiggles in the ubiquitous dust. He muttered something about ghosts but didn't elaborate. He'd already had enough of such that day.

At one level he relaxed a little. Len Verran kept snorting, "Bugger-all here!" as he sniffed in doorways, venturing no farther but standing there and making disapproving comments about whatever history they had contained. Davey had the distinct impression the little man hated that house, whether he now thought he owned it or not.

In possible atonement for the sloth of her spouse, Hilda Verran nosed, ratlike, around each chamber, not failing to examine a single item for the whereabouts of the precious piece of paper. He watched her ample bum bob about the dark corners and crevices of the vast master bedroom—lately inhabited, they each told him separately, by Hannah—and then rummage through the four-poster with its mound of unmade bedclothes at the foot of the mattress, dating from God knew when.

Every now and then the Tintagel lady threw him a suspicious glance, as if fearing he had already found the document and had immediately concealed it on his person. When Davey wasn't the object of her hostile attention, she would turn and growl at her husband for his loud oaths and his continued mutterings through clenched teeth about an ungrateful hussy given to inveterate lying and—more interestingly to the Canadian visitor—of a house soured in every pore by the presence for so many years of two female viragos, locked in hate and bereft of the healthy balancing presence of men.

That kind of comment made Davey realize that the little sod from Tintagel actually had a lively grasp of his family's history, perhaps considerably more than he did, especially of that part of it centred in the damp stone space of Lanoe, which perched so impudently on the very edge of the wind- and rain-lashed moor.

Even at this stage, at least intermittently, Hilda appeared anxious to maintain some degree of civility with Davey. A stance, he decided, that was informed by her sense of caution—just in case he and they should end up in adversarial positions over the possible bequeathals from those rich overseas sources he'd invented when it would need all her powers of persuasion to get him to divvy them up.

By the time they had "done" Aunt Nora's bedroom, skipped through two ice-cold bathrooms, and started toward the two attic rooms with their magnificent views of the open moor beyond the currently overgrown gardens, he had come up with a further plan to keep this odd little couple out of his hair. Or at least to get them out of the picture while he investigated Lanoe in peace and made some discreet inquiries in the village about these so-called cousins from Tintagel and maybe learn more about his deceased aunt who was linking him with them from her freshly dug grave.

His scheme was a simple one. As they'd climbed up the last flight of narrow stairs to the top of the house, he'd fingered something small and hard in the large pocket of the raincoat he was still wearing. Moving quickly ahead of them to take advantage of the light from the small dormer window, he whipped out the object and examined it. Grubby and somewhat bent, it proved to be a piece of card with the words PIRATES OF PENZANCE and some letters and numbers running along its frayed edge. He instantly summoned up the visit he and Ken had made the previous winter to a disastrous performance of that particular Gilbert and Sullivan operetta in Seattle.

He put a few further paces between himself and the puffing Verrans before holding up the fragment of ticket stub to the window and tearing off the fragment containing the words PIRATES OF before stuffing the scrap back into his pocket. He now had his makeshift plan in some coherence. All he needed was a place to enact it and that he didn't discover until it was almost too late!

They had entered the very room where, sixty years earlier, hot little hands had clasped frozen toes and a small boy had refused to listen to the strange noises coming from his Uncle Joseph's garden or the Devil's own moor. Refusing the rising images, he rushed over to the windowsill and shoved the ticket stump behind the frayed velvet curtains that had hung there, he reflected wonderingly, for most of his life. The diminutive couple pushed and shoved each other to be first around the foot of the brass bedstead when he emitted a whoop of phony discovery and made his excited announcement.

"My God! Look what I've found! Not the will, exactly, but the old girl's secret, I'd swear to that!"

Davey thought Hilda was about to expire—at least to faint—as her ample body curves shook and sweat broke out on the pored expanse of her face and mottled neck. "What *be* it then, Mr. Bryant? What on earth have 'ee been and found?"

He handed the ticket to her just as her husband's arm reached out to grab it. Hilda should be the recipient, Davey had decided, as she had evidenced the most cupidity right from the start.

"She sometimes spoke when visiting us in Canada of her dear friend Rosemary," he began. "She lived, as I recall, in Marazion, directly across from St. Michael's Mount. Hannah would stay with her whenever she was doing business in Penzance. Now this can hardly be coincidence. I bet dollars to doughnuts that the bank vault in nearby Penzance has all her secret accounts tucked away. Just like dear old Auntie to keep that stuff as far away from home as possible. Yes, that was Hannah for you."

Hilda scowled her suspicion as greed and incredulity fought within her. "She b'aint made no mention of this woman, have her, Len?"

"*That* one!" Len harrumphed. "She wouldn't have told her own mother where her was to! Allus a sly one. Her only talked when her wanted something out on 'ee. True to her type and different from the rest on us what is 'family.' No wonder her sister-in-law hated her. And we was always told up to Tintagel as her cousins that she were no good to her husband, neither. That were pretty ways ago, o' course. But the poor bugger died without never knowing her wifely consolations, if you do catch my meaning."

Hilda obviously thought her spouse was going too far. "Oi don' think our cousin wants to hear all that stuff, Len. O' course, she were always sweet with us, you, seeing as how, Len and me being her second cousins, we all shared a grandmother. Well, 'twere her grandmother-*in-law*, Oi s'pose, what with her being outside blood and that. She trusted us, you see, loike no one else. Then who else were there to tend 'un during them terrible months when her was failin'? When we was her only kin and she thought the whole village was against her?"

"Which, o' course, they was," her husband added with evident satisfaction. "That's why we got her out of this great barn and into the Breakers and was pleased to meet the huge expense. Not all do know that, Oi reckon. We, her Tintagel cousins, paid a pretty penny, which Oi don't expect no Penzance money can meet!"

Davey began to panic that they were getting away from the ticket stub and his scheme. He waved the former before them. "I tell you what. I'll drive on down there in a day or so and see what I can find out. Well worth checking, to my mind."

That did the trick. They were almost bobbing up and down in excitement.

"We could all on us go down together. Maike it a proper ole family outin'. With Hannah so close to us all, it would be nice for us to know the rest of her family better." Little Hilda licked her lips before elaborating. "Now it all comes back to Oi! Yessir! She *did* mention some Rosemary person. Don' 'ee remember, Len? Oi bide her come up here once to Pentudy. Pretty little thing her was, if Oi do remember aroight. Can't remember her address, though."

Davey smiled to himself. Her memory was indeed performing miraculously, considering he'd just invented said Rosemary of Marazion. As for dear Aunt Hannah utilizing a bank vault in Penzance, his suspicion was she'd have far more likely shoved any secret papers or whatnot under a granite boulder up there on the moor. Not that for a moment he thought she had. Far more likely, if she'd had something to hide, she'd have secreted it in the perpetually dim world of that rambling stone house. And if such had been the case, these petite but indefatigable "vacuum cleaners" would have long ago sucked it out.

Hilda smirked. "Would 'ee be having her address then? Oi b'aint sure Oi wrote of un down when us moved dear Aunt Hannah into the Breakers and Oi knew she wouldn' be seeing people from outside no more."

Davey met her cocked glance. "I'm pretty sure she said it was near the vicarage," he lied. "I'll ask the vicar when I get there."

This was followed by a small silence in the cramped little bedroom. Davey could hear the rasp of breathing from two small throats, and realized the diminutive duo had picked up immediately on his implicit repudiation of the "family outing" notion.

"Well, we got bravun many things to do around here now she'm gone. Would 'ee let on us know if you do turn anything up?"

"There's a pile of bills sittin' round still awaitin' to be paid," her husband added. "A few o' they dollars would come in useful, they would."

Davey decided his lure needed bigger bait. "We could be thinking in millions," he mused aloud. "But there's no good just speculating. I think I'll go down on the weekend and spend as long as it takes. Rosemary used to accompany Aunt Hannah on the bank-vault visits so she should prove *very* useful." He smiled genially at them. But the reason for his rictus was pride in his continuing powers of invention.

The Verrans could hardly wait to get downstairs and, Davey was convinced, get in hot pursuit of that El Dorado. Waving from the front door, he watched them scurry down the path. He imagined the covetous couple would skip supper at Lanoe—though their excuse for now leaving was to fetch supplies for just that—and roar south in their Morris Mini. For what was mere hunger compared with greed? As they drove away in a sea of waving arms, he closed the door of Lanoe behind him, ready now for the several tasks he had set himself in the village where Hannah had spent most of her long if unhappy life. Not least was to investigate their claim to kinship that in the light of his never having heard of them before he was sure would prove bogus.

FIVE

I t wasn't the greed of the Verrans that led Davey into Pentudy church the very next morning. But it wasn't anything particularly exalted, either. True, he had been irritated by their facile air of knowledge over their purported cousin and was keen to have more details about his aunt than they might have. But also guiding his feet toward the potential repository of village knowledge in its parish church was a string of embarrassing images from his hebetic past, the time when as a curmudgeonly child he had sniggered and smirked in the pew with his cousin, Jan, as a fresh-minted Hannah stomped down the aisle on the arm of his father to the altar steps where Uncle Joseph awaited. His uncle was bereft of a best man, but as surrogate was Joseph's sister, Nora, who stood there holding a single lily, looking like something out of *The Grapes of Wrath* as she awaited the arrival of the woman who was to take her brother away and give her a more precarious role now that she'd no longer be the chatelaine of Lanoe.

It was Aunt Nora's baleful presence, Davey now decided sixty years later, that had made Uncle Joseph twitch and dance on the broad flagstones like a distraught schoolboy, rather than reflect the comportment of a distinguished war veteran, a middle-aged yeoman farmer who had finally bowed to family pressure and sought a wife.

On that warm fall day, apart from summoning up that razor-edged icon from a distant past, Davey was impervious to the general history of St. Brychan's. He ignored the worm-holed oaken stocks ranged along the church's porch since Tudor times and, once inside, passed under the seventeenth-century flag of Charles II, given to his Royalist villagers by a grateful monarch after the Cornishly hated Civil War, and which had hung proudly ever since upon the Norman walls above the great west doors.

Skirting the granite baptismal font where his own infant shape, and his father's squirming baby body, plus those of countless ancestors before them, had been held on high by priestly hands over the cold water, he headed for the adjacent bell tower in which were suspended the ropes that made the clanging campanology of Christ echo across the valley and over the moor each Sabbath morn and evening, again on every High Saint's Day, and perhaps pealing especially madly for weddings and conversely tolling more sombrely and slowly when they rang out for the dead.

But it wasn't the bells he sought, much as he missed their weekly presence in his now-Canadian ears, but a large ledger that he knew used to be kept by Father Trewin in a deep recess in the rough granite wall of the Norman tower. He was looking for *The Parish Register*, in which the old priest had once proudly shown the visiting choirboys from the neighbouring parish handwritten entries going back to the eighteenth century.

Quickly he found what he was searching for. Evidently Father Trewin's several successors continued to use his place for the leather-bound tome. From above a thin layer of bat and mouse droppings he withdrew one of the three heavy volumes that were stacked in the musky dark. The one he selected was a record of weddings.

Those he ignored were entries for baptisms and funerals—all of them across the span of centuries.

The entry he was after and found was for May 20, 1940. It went as follows: "Joseph Petherick Bryant, Bachelor of Lanoe House in the parish of Pentudy, after the third time of asking, was wedded in this Church of Saint Brychan to Hannah Ursula Bandon, Spinster, of the Parish of Saint Mary's in the London Borough of Stoke Newington."

Bending over the fine copperplate, he pursed his lips with satisfaction. His first step had been achieved. He now had written proof of Aunt Hannah's formal link with the family and didn't have to rely on a child's uncertain memory. And this was ages, of course, before she could ever have heard of the Verrans and their not-so-subtle inferences that they had a claim on her. On thinking of those two, he jotted down his aunt's maiden name and the London church, thinking he would call on Alyson if for some reason that information required further corroboration.

That done he replaced the volume and hastened outside to the fullness of day. He told himself that things were going well, but all the same he was pleased to escape the bottled past and its yeasty implications.

At first he decided to return to the Cornish Arms and have an early lunch before possibly driving to Tintagel and checking comparable church records to those he'd just examined, though this time on the *baptismal* backgrounds to Len and Hilda Verran, so as to ascertain just how closely related to his aunt they really were, if at all. But as he retraced his steps, a different idea occurred to him. He would stop in at the vicarage and see what he could learn from the present incumbent, not only about the last days of his old aunt's moorland existence but how the Verrans had featured in them.

Hannah being a Methodist, her nephew suspected, would be no major obstacle. If the vicar himself proved to be imported from north of the River Tamar—a tendency Davey assumed had grown since the consonant "Englishing" of the Duchy he had despondently observed in driving there—then priest and widow could have more in common than their differing denominations suggested. He was hoping it would thus prove to be.

In Davey's opinion such shared circumstances as both being outsiders could engender a common zeal transcending religious loyalty, much as radically dissimilar experiences and backgrounds with their concomitant ignorance could just as easily fuel hate. If fortune smiled on him, then it would turn out to be the former situation.

But before reaching the large Georgian vicarage with its adjacent copse of tall elms housing what he could already make out as a large and noisy rookery, something happened that was to make Pentudy's priest not his first but his second live witness to the old lady's fading embers of life at Lanoe. He was making his way along a narrow stone footbridge bordering a wide if shallow ford bifurcating the gravel road when his attention was riveted by a loud shout.

"Hey, you! Would 'ee give on a hand, please?"

Davey found the source to be coming from quite close to the bridge he was traversing—from an elderly man with long white hair escaping from under a large brimmed and sweat-stained hat. The man was beckoning fiercely to Davey with one hand while with the other he pointed at the antique contraption he appeared to be lugging through the languid waters of the stream that circled the village and broadened into the aforementioned ford at that point.

The old fellow was either stuck or physically exhausted, but not so much of the latter as to prevent him continuing to holler and gesticulate as Davey hurried across the bridge and returned to the bizarre figure by daintily using convenient stepping stones that barely surfaced the mud-brown water. It wasn't until then that Davey realized the old man was hauling a large tricycle, itself roped to a wooden construction containing at its centre an immense stone wheel. It reminded him of those monster circles of Stilton cheese or Dutch Edam to be found in specialty shops back in Vancouver.

Davey seized the other side of the machine's handlebars and, bracing in unison, they started to haul the heavy weight to dry land. Not until they had stopped, both panting, and Davey had eyed his companion's dripping conveyance, did he realize the nature of the heavy object they'd been lugging. Behind the tricycle proved to be a mobile knife grinder, consisting of a crude wheel of granite connected to a primitive cast-iron handle to make it spin. Davey hadn't seen the likes of this contraption since immigrating to Canada and entering an era when blunt or worn knives were often discarded and new ones bought in their place. There had been a hardware store in Vancouver that supplied a sharpening service, but Joseph William Clemo, as the old man quickly informed Davey was his full name, went house-to-house performing the task. Out of the blue he added the information that he was on the way to the vicarage to supply his regular service;. in fact, would have been there that very moment had he not misjudged the recent rains and the consequent rise in the waters of the ford.

The old chap—Davey decided he couldn't have been less than eighty—then eyed his helper up and down, digesting both accent and clothes before asking where he was from. Hannah's nephew informed him that he now lived in Canada but that he had been born in nearby St. Keverne though having strong Pentudy connections.

Clemo took his time to absorb that, and made but one comment. "Well, today's world is full of strangers, Oi can tell 'ee that!" Then he added obliquely that Pentudy seemed to be full of strangers, too. That said, the fellow returned to questioning, wanting to know what Davey was doing in Pentudy, followed by inquiring whether he had such a thing as a penknife that needed sharpening.

Before Davey could elaborate on his aunt's death as the reason for his presence and the fact that he had no penknife, the knife grinder was looking beyond him as if a prospective customer might materialize out of thin air. Somewhat taken aback, Davey hastily threw out a question of his own, anxious to utilize this potential repository of local information before he disappeared. Had the old man, by any chance, known his late aunt? Had he maybe visited Lanoe on his knife-grinding?

In seconds Davey saw he'd scored a bull's-eye!

"Knew'd the old girl well, Oi did. 'Cos her weren't originally from here but come long ago. Now that testy sister-in-law of her'n was born to Pentudy and never let t'other forget it! 'Twere a bad day when Oi come off the moor from Bolventor and they was at it, which were most of the toime, Oi'm tellin' of 'ee. If Oi were to talk to one then that were it! No ways Oi was goin' get the ear of t'other. Ran two households under one roof, that's what they Bryant women did. Sharpened knives for both in me toime and 'twere like armin' two bloody Boadiceas," he added, nodding fiercely. "Oi some-toimes thought mebbe Oi wasn't the roight person to be visiting of 'em. They was well enough armoured wi' their tongues!"

Davey thought it time to nudge the garrulous old fellow to fresh pastures, but Clemo forestalled him. "Then Oi s'pose you knew'd of her well, too. Funny, Oi b'aint seed's 'ee to Pentudy before. Then Oi reckon Oi wouldn', you being a stranger and that."

"She visited us regularly in Canada. Almost yearly and almost up to the end. As a matter of fact, I knew Pentudy well when I was a little boy. Did part of my growing up here when my uncle was alive. As well as St. Keverne where I was born. Aunt Hannah first came here as my Uncle Joseph's bride, and I attended her wedding." He broke off, half expecting Clemo would refuse to believe he was old enough, but the knife grinder's thoughts were already elsewhere.

"Bet you wasn't sure 'twere she when her turned up at your place with her faice all bit up after ole Gypo had a go at her. Moind you, that were part 'cos they two women was still spattin'. That's why the dog went out on his moind and savaged her, see? 'Mazed, the poor bugger were, because she thought she were his mistress and Miss Nora thought likewise and he were confused. That do happen wi' they overbreds, specially red setters. Half-crazed he was, too, from the overexercisin'. Who wouldn' be, moind, what wi' that long-legged Nora stridin' miles and miles over the moor wid 'un in the morning and then ole Hannah competin' by doin' the same with him in th' arternoons? Why, Oi seed 'un halfway up Rough Tor at teatoime when they still had five mile or so to walk back to Lanoe. Fred Pengelly, the postman over to Bolventor, *many* toimes told Oi how he'd seed that poor pantin' Gypo with his other woman, that Nora, all the way to Pendennis Barrow before the sun were full up!"

Davey tried another tack. "The Verrans were saying something of the sort."

The veteran knife grinder cleared his throat and aimed a heavy gob back into the ford he'd recently navigated. "Don' 'ee heed they buggers! What do 'em know but what they been told in the village? Come from Tintagel way, they say. Reckon to be cousins of the ole girl. There's some say they b'aint little folk be accident but is bewitched by piskies. Not that Oi do go for all that super-bloody-stition. But they surely stuck like stoats to ole Hannah when they reckoned she were goin' out on her moind. Reckon it were worth on it for 'em, too. They got Lanoe House, didn' 'em? And moved in so soon as 'ee could say Jack Robinson!"

"There's a dispute about that," Davey said quickly. "They'll get their due portion if it's proved legally correct. It's my understanding the house has to be divvied up between Hannah Bryant's two extant relatives. Then she herself was only a part owner in the first place, even if she had title to live there. I have a strong suspicion there's no way any of it will go to those avaricious Lilliputians."

Clemo might have been a stranger to Jonathan Swift's land of Lilliput, but he was in no doubt as to whom Davey was referring. "Well, keep your hair on, boyo! They two is nothing but busybodies and leechin' for easy money. Proper ole scandal in the village when they took her over, as it were, and moved into the big house. Though ole Hannah were no friend of most of they in Pentudy, they was sorry for her when they squeezed her out and put her in that there Breakers home for oldies up to Tintagel. Not that Oi reckon they got much. Bit from that weirdy vicar who went and bought her car off 'em behind her back. Bloody Christians! Oi wouldn' trust none of 'em—neither Methodies like her was and they, to that Father Laws-Johnston and his bloody bishop—further than Oi can spit!"

Davey had just witnessed the man's prowess in that direction but refrained from commenting on it. Instead he asked, "Father Laws-Johnston wouldn't have had much to do with her, would he? Her being a Methodist and that?"

Clemo shot him an odd glance from beneath the brim of that ever more warlocky-looking hat. "Now Oi wouldn' be sayin' that," he said, his words heavy with meaning. "Hannah and that bugger had something in common aroight. Only 'twere nothing to do wi' religion. Gospel truth is they was both bloody snobs. They both hated Pentudy as if 'twere full of writhin' adders! 'Twere the same ole tricks wi' Father Harris afore 'un. You mark my words! She got on wi' they vicars aroight. Some do say more than you might imagine from a widow…"

Davey couldn't restrain himself. "Just because she didn't have a Cornish accent?" he remonstrated. "And presumably, neither the vicar? Surely that's nothing but the worst kind of village gossip."

Clemo shrugged, not at all taken aback. "Have it which way, maister! But Oi heard report of her being seen goin' into the vicarage when most folks is sleepin'—and ditto for the cassocks slippin' into Lanoe House when others is done for the day. Course, that were a year or two back."

This was a brand-new image of Davey's aunt. He had always accorded her a pristine state in spite of her marital status. Not that her virginity or lack of it was something he'd ever been disposed to dwell on. But in his adolescent shying away from such topics—probably fortified by his growing gay sensibilities—he had felt that

Hannah had owned to the same measure of crisp "nonsexiness" as her archrival, his presumably virgin Aunt Nora, whom he assumed was regarded even by her village detractors (who thought her hoity-toity) as someone forever and ferociously in possession of an intact hymen.

Aunt Hannah's sex life—a wholly new panorama opened for Davey under the aegis of old Joseph William Clemo! From having no concept he was suddenly prepared to view his aunt as a would-be "harlot of the moor," conjuring up an image of progressively frustrated sex mildewing in loneliness as she wandered from bracken to boulder across the barren moor.

But Davey's informant wasn't about to permit him lewd fantasies in that direction. "'Cos Oi allus say she were more sinned against than a sinner, you. Not just that cold bitch of a sister-in-law, neither. Went back long before *that*." In good Cornish fashion he stretched *that* for a full three syllables: *tha-a-a-at*. "Goes back to poor ole Joe Bryant himself. Did 'ee know as how your uncle were bravun wounded to Flanders Fields?"

"We were told as children," Davey acknowledged, "that he was one of the first to get mustard gas. It was that which eventually killed him."

"That weren' the half on it, maister. Gassin' of 'un caused the retchin' and spittin', but 'tweren' that what took his *manhood*. 'Twere a piece o' shrapnel twixt his legs what did that to 'un. Oi had that from ole Doctor Apse over to Delabole who were his doctor. Oi used to do his knives, too," he added somewhat superfluously. "Joe was no good to the women, married or no."

To that laconic observation Davey had no immediate answer. Instead he took to his uncle's defence. "Uncle Joseph certainly didn't act like some kind of eunuch. He did the work of three men around Lanoe, my father used to say. And he worshipped the ground Aunt Hannah walked on. Even a kid could see that."

The old man shrugged again. "Oi b'aint *disputin'*—jest *explainin'*— what her didn' get and why it did make her what it did. And her havin' that nasty Nora loathin' her under the same roof was no help, Oi can tell 'ee!"

Something told Davey he was going to get no more from the garrulous knife grinder. Then he felt he really didn't want any more tittle-tattle. He'd already been provided with enough to mull on. Uncle Joseph devoid of balls, Aunt Nora unrelenting in hate, and Aunt Hannah fevered with unrequited lust seeking sexual rather than sacerdotal relief from her village priests…

"You paint a weirdo picture of my family," he told the old man. "An impotent uncle and a sex-starved wife—" He caught himself in time. Clemo was watching him suspiciously, his shaggy brows thickening into one bushy line. Davey grew afraid the knife grinder thought he was mocking him in refuting his revelations.

"But the truth is, Mr. Clemo, I'm grateful for what you've told me. I stayed on after the funeral, you see, precisely to find out anything I could about my aunt. I was fond of her, you know, in spite of her funny ways. I knew she was terribly unhappy every time she visited us, and I was determined to find out why exactly. You've helped me a lot, so thank you."

The old chap seemed a little mollified. "Oi only tells what Oi knows and that only to them what Oi respect. You helped Oi through the ford, and bein' a perfect stranger and that. Oi don' forget them things, maister. You can ask any on these buggers to Pentudy and around. They'll tell 'ee that Joseph William Clemo, the knife grinder, b'aint one to forget a kindness."

Being bareheaded, Davey touched his forehead before turning away. To his surprise Clemo responded by placing filthy-nailed fingers to his broad felt brim. The mutual salutation suggested they were now companions of some kind, though Davey wasn't sure of quite what.

"See you around," he called back as he once more headed for the vicarage to elicit what he felt certain would be much less exciting information. But Davey had the odd sensation he wouldn't be seeing his knife grinder again.

Six

Father Hector Laws-Johnston was at first cagey, to say the least. Davey remembered English reticence, but this was something else! The vicar talked to him in the gloom of the hallway, which in the damp mottling of its unpapered walls reminded him forcibly of the one other house of substance in the moorland village—Lanoe. It was quite obvious the priest didn't relish his presence, and equally, that he regarded not only the person of the Canadian visitor's aunt, but also her memory, as part of the uncomfortable price he had to pay as the incumbent of such an ingrown and impoverished parish.

Standing there, slight Davey was uncomfortably aware the vicar towered over him. Six foot seven was his estimate, but the height was given further emphasis by the fact the gaunt figure was clad in a black soutane. The priest's visitor also noticed that the clerical garment was markedly stained down its buttoned front and frayed at the cuffs. Nor did the sense of penury stop there. Even in the charitably dim light, his dog collar seemed more yellow than white.

Davey concluded the vicar was by no means prosperous, and that softened his antagonism at the priest's frosty hostility and utter refusal to unbend before charm or even politeness.

It was the Aunt Hannah connection that Davey pushed. In vain he stressed their consanguinity, their friendship as nephew and aunt, her frequent visits to them in recent years. Then, as backup, he threw in his pubescent presence at her wedding and his lengthy familiarity with both Lanoe House and Pentudy. He was almost out of breath when he was through.

Father Laws-Johnston acknowledged all that with a most unpriestly grunt—in fact, it was first cousin to a belch—followed by a gruff speculation as to what any of that might have to do with him.

Davey decided to pull out more trenchant stops. "The purpose of my continuing presence in Pentudy, Father, is to investigate my aunt's last years here and her subsequent death in an old people's home—the Breakers at Poltiddy. She suddenly stopped writing either to me or to my cousin in London during the past year or so, and we were both rather puzzled. Then, at the funeral service yesterday, I met a couple from here who—not to put it too finely—filled me with suspicion. I got the distinct impression they were exploiting her during her last days and that their only real interest was in the money they assumed she had."

Davey wasn't sure what prompted him to add to that. Perhaps the fear he smelled lurking beneath the be-cassocked presence. Perhaps he'd read too many recent accounts of priestly pedophiles back in Canada. Or again perhaps he suddenly summoned up memories of a tall clergyman scoutmaster tenderly feeling him up when his parish troop was camping on those selfsame moors.

"I'm thinking of calling in the police," he lied, for he had no intention of doing anything of the sort, sharing the usual gay distrust of the arm of the law.

As with Joseph William Clemo, Davey again hit the jackpot. In the feeble light the cleric seemed to decrease an inch or two. He swayed as if hit by a bullet, and finally his tongue loosened in a wordy English way.

"Oh, come, Mr. Bryant! The Verrans aren't quite as bad as that! They may be bewitched by the scent of wealth. I remember the harsh bargain they struck in selling me your aunt's, or rather your Uncle Joseph's old Austin 6, which had been lying there for years in that drafty stable since long before I came to the parish. And they do make a nuisance of themselves, stirring up trouble in the village by inventing a lot of gossip of one kind or another. But though that may well make them objectionable in the eyes of the Almighty, I doubt whether it makes them criminals in the eyes of Man."

But Davey wasn't about to be put off. "I wasn't thinking only of their avarice but of the implications of what they said after the service when we all three explored Lanoe for the will they seemed convinced my aunt had hidden there. If they were to be believed, my aunt might have suffered spells of madness. The death of my Aunt Nora, her sister-in-law, might have come about as a result of the two of them quarrelling violently in jealousy over a dog, an Irish setter they apparently shared. Then again—and here I have other sources, too—they suggested that in her fits of depression, or whatever, she was prone to throw herself at the local clergy—"

The reply was instant enough. "May I remind you we are talking about an exceedingly old lady. I suspect senility rather than insanity was her problem in those last days."

Davey switched horses immediately. "All the more reason she needed protection, I would've thought. We're constantly reading of doctors persuading elderly patients to change their wills to their own selfish advantage. Perhaps something of that sort happened here. In any case, it won't hurt if the police take a look. Too much of this kind of thing going on, if you ask me, especially in a country like Great Britain with its increasingly aging population."

It was a hobbyhorse he had aired quite a lot back home, but now he faltered. True, he was certainly suspicious about a lot of things concerning his aunt, and he increasingly disliked the dwarfs who had battened onto her, but the paramount reason was the sight of this wiry, willowy man beginning to wilt like a thirsty tulip on the muddied slates of the vicarage hallway. Davey realized he had unwittingly found a weak spot in someone who had initially come on as full of arrogant asperity and was quite prepared to slough him off.

God knew why the priest had been transformed by the mere evoking of the police, the Canadian thought. Perhaps he had deflowered every youth in Pentudy and screwed his aunt to boot! Of one thing Davey was certain: if he persisted in cruelly playing with the man, exploiting his frailties, threatening him with visits from the authorities, then he would be acting no better than those who had ranged themselves against Aunt Hannah. No better than the avaricious Verrans, or those unknowns in the village whom the knife grinder had hinted had compounded her isolation of which she had complained unceasingly through those cracked, dry lips for so many years of her life.

He sucked in breath and changed the subject. "Earlier this morning I went to the bell tower to find the parish registers," he told the vicar. "I knew where they were since I was a choirboy over in St. Keverne. I looked up my uncle and aunt's wedding entry and discovered she was originally from a London parish."

If Davey had sucked in breath, Father Laws-Johnston hissed it out. "Oh, I could have told you that right away. That was the weirdest coincidence. I did my curacy in Stoke Newington—that was my first title. She told me she was from there."

A suspicion of a smile flitted across the face of the elderly priest, and Davey knew he felt out of immediate danger. "She never told me at first that she was a ward of the parish, though. Did you know, Mr. Bryant, that your aunt was what the Victorians would have called a foundling?"

It was the visitor's turn to almost stumble. "I did not. Then I think there's an awful lot I don't know still, one way or another. You think you know someone reasonably well and you don't at all."

"How true, Mr. Bryant! How true for us all!"

And with that observation the tall and still-mysterious cleric led Davey to his front door and a return to that brisk fall day—to chew on the fact that, among other things, Aunt Hannah was probably a bastard. It made him feel, for one thing, that nothing was really quite what it seemed. Perhaps there were things about himself he didn't know, things he would be rudely shocked to find out. And there was that altered Cornwall all about him. Once he had been so *certain* as to what was what. Then that had all changed behind his back. Now he was sure of nothing.

Davey shivered and made himself think of the plans ahead. He was beginning to think that either the "new" Cornwall or his returning self had land mines scattered in every direction. He would try to stay on safe paths.

SEVEN

It had been Davey's intention to have a leisurely lunch at the Cornish Arms where he could mull over the morning's experiences and then head for Tintagel's Public Library and Registry Office to spend the afternoon checking on the claims and the backgrounds of the Verrans. However, it was not to be. Drawn up in the car park, adjacent to his own rented car, was an enormous white vehicle that not only virtually filled the whole space but seemed to have people swarming from various parts of it. He recognized what it was immediately: a kind of truck-bus hybrid common back in Vancouver, a movie vehicle employed both to lug film equipment or serve as accommodation for participating actors and technicians. Davey turned away disconsolate, made gloomy at this further indication of exploitation of a venue he had once called home and always thought holy.

Mechanically he downed a pasty made on the premises and which he would otherwise have enjoyed, toyed with a tankard of cider, then returned to the assembled movie trucks to skulk in the hope that one of the men who had been sitting at the surrounding tables in the pub's public bar would drop a hint as to why they were there in that remote village. He soon discovered they were a TV crew who'd arrived that very day to make a drama series or a doc-umentary—he wasn't sure which—and that it involved lots of moorland footage; fabled Dozmary Pool, home to the sword, Excalibur, to the east; and also a substantial degree of King Arthur's Tintagel, including the cave where the mythical Merlin was said to have lived. His hearing quickened when he heard the name Tintagel, but it was something physical, more like an electric prod up his rear, when he realized the crew were making a TV series based on an amalgam of the various Arthurian legends only updated to the present. A series that involved the dwarf Frocin and something about an evil astrologer dwarf who may or may not have been one and the same person.

Davey's body was now shaking. Like St. Paul's conversion on the way to Damascus, like a burst of light and a toll of thunder in a tropical storm, the conviction entered him that the Verrans were in some way—in a manner he had yet to fathom—a reincarnation of the medieval Frocin. Now two instead of one, now venal and prosaic in their instincts, but come direct in their shrivelled shapes down the chute of time: still of Tintagel, still bent on evildoing...

As the thoughts reverberated through him like the clash of bells, he fled the moviemakers and their equipment and headed upward to the moors where, he now decided in a frantic moment, enlight-enment might yet be found. The visit to Tintagel to investigate the Verrans' background could wait. He was now convinced the eternal, mysterious moor would provide more. Besides, he needed respite from what he was rapidly beginning to believe was a malevolent rev-elation from the remote past that was yet connected to his aunt's death and unhappy life.

His pace slackened as he climbed over the last rough-hewn stone wall of some farmer's forlorn gesture at cultivation, and he welcomed the fresh, breezy fingers into his thinning white hair. If he was glad he'd left his tweed cap on the vehicle's front seat, he was equally happy that, in spite of the sun, he'd retained his rain-coat for warmth.

Before he returned to moviemaking and dwarfs he desperately wanted to be filled with the spirit of place. He made himself look up at the sweep of sky, so achingly familiar from when as a small, lithe body he had danced under it sixty years earlier, free of the current encumbrance of arthritis. With a stiffened gait now, and distance-watering eyes, he fed on compact clouds as they scudded toward the sun-silvered curves of the Camel Estuary at Padstow and subsequently cross the tiny gleam of Atlantic beyond Trevose light-house, a previous childhood treasure of the night. Equally familiar a lifetime later was the tawny sweep of moorland dotted with dolmens, where timid ponies snorted from a distance and black-faced sheep baaed in apprehension at the sight of human kind.

Between the crater of Rough Tor and the steep flanks of Brown Willy, he feasted on the heather and bracken as it made an ochroid unity amid dull clumps of green gorse with its year-round pips of yellow. He shivered. But he was unaware whether that was the response of his aging blood to the cool vigour of the moorland wind or a tremor of delight as he accepted the spell of this beloved land-scape, where the unique russet of peat glowed as the sudden lips of gurgling rivulets and of such streams that were eventually to become the major Cornish waterways of the Fowey and the Camel.

But it wasn't all pastoral lyricism. He climbed a neighbouring outcropping where he remembered what could be seen looking east. It wasn't only the abrupt finger of a granite monolith that again greeted his eyes, but he could remember what was inscribed upon it: the bleak account of a distraught Matthew Weeks murdering his sweetheart, Charlotte Dymond, on that lonely spot in 1844.

When he turned his back on that sad little saga of long-ago lovers, it was to look fully in the opposite direction. But this aspect was no longer the same as he had known as a boy. Instead of the two small replicas of the dazzling white pyramids of slag heaped from the China clay surrounding St. Austell there now sprouted six or seven disfiguring interlopers on the face of the moor, a visage that had hitherto not changed radically for human eyes since the First Bronze Age.

He turned quickly from that prospect, not desiring to repeat the sensations of the previous day when journeying from the chapel on the headland through the tourist-driven dreck of contemporary Cornwall. Nor was he ready yet to contend with the updated Frocins. He just wanted to lose himself, as Hannah apparently had, in that boulder-and-bracken wilderness, along with her crazed dog, Gypo, as they sought to escape both the venom within Lanoe and the bile of Pentudy in the tumble and toss of soaring ravens with their basso croaks, the feline mews of buzzards, and the sight of the rabbits bobbing their tails in flight before she and Gypo. All of that was more than a shadow and a smell.

But the escape from self, from the imprisonment of dark thoughts, wasn't arrived at so facilely as by the provision of a string of feral images, the panorama of an ancient land replete with magnificent views, or the comfortable knowledge that one's youth was cradled in it all.

In the midst of the soft tinkle and purple glow of the ubiquitous heather, Davey gave up. He had been aiming for the violent metaphor of a particular moorland bog, something that in its bright green deception as solidity could prove a grim receptacle of those who walked unsuspecting over its surface and sunk in the bottomless mud. He wanted to stand safe on the squelchy peat and imagine the flailing arms and strangled cries as a victim was sucked under to suffocate in the stranglehold of soft, slimy earth. Davey wondered if that hadn't been Hannah's image of the moor. She had only spoken to him with affection of the unfettered land beyond Lanoe, but it occurred to him as he skirted the piled megaliths of unknown purpose from an ancient past that perhaps she had wished to put him off the scent because Aunt Nora had always been such a verbose—according to Hannah—admirer of the moor. And the two simply struggled in competitiveness for its alluring spell.

But this was a path he didn't want to descend. He suddenly changed his tracks, refusing the menace of the bog legend that flourished wherever the moor obtained, and shifted reluctantly instead to the matter of Hannah and the clues that a return to her house might give. So he retraced the five or six miles he had undergone and, while vaguely trying to recollect the significance in Cornish lore of the presence of three magpies who sat on a boulder eyeing him, started mentally to compose a letter that would probably end up as a phone call to both Ken and Cousin Alyson as to the true identity of the Verrans.

EIGHT

Driving to Wadebridge, Hilda Verran forcibly argued that a trip to Penzance and Marazion at that particular point was a daft enterprise. She declared over and over again that they only had the Canadian's utterances to go on and that he was obviously in Cornwall to see what he could get out of his aunt's death. She stressed that the legitimacy of his claim—along with that of the unknown Cousin Alyson—to Lanoe House was something they knew only from *his* lips and not from any legal document they'd seen. Come to that, she told her husband, she wasn't even sure there *was* an Alyson in London. Why, indeed, should they take on trust this white-haired stranger who seemed to change his accents at the drop of a hat? Was he, in fact, the selfsame nephew whom his aunt said patronized her under the guise of entertaining her, and who had succeeded in persuading their cousin on her last trip that she should make no more journeys to Canada where they only surreptitiously made fun of her?

But although Len had nodded reluctantly in agreement as she

said these things, they weren't the decisive factors that changed his mind. They had almost reached the medieval bridge leading over the Camel into Wadebridge when Hilda happened to express anxiety over leaving the Canadian interloper to wander freely about Lanoe, choosing whatever he wanted to take and perhaps getting into some mischievous alliance with all those villagers who had so hated Hannah and from whose spiteful tongues she and Len had so often protected the old woman.

It was that which had done it. He'd suddenly wrenched the steering wheel of the little van until they were heading toward Egloshayle and ultimately Bodmin. "You'm roight, maid! Us don' want him to be prowlin' around to Pentudy while we is off on some bloody wild-goose chase. Never did loike the look on him, you. What wi' they quick-movin' eyes and that fast tongue. All the maikin's of a rogue, roight there, you!"

She had let him go on like that all the way along the snaking Camel Valley, though hoping he'd eventually quiet down for the business of shopping when they reached the busy market town. It was also necessary to have her irascible mate in a more or less tractable frame of mind by the time they got back to Pentudy that evening.

When the Verrans returned from Bodmin, though, it was to find Pentudy abuzz with the presence of TV crews and their impedimenta. Len thought he saw the insignia of the BBC emblazoned on a hand-held camera. He at once suggested they delay their return to Lanoe House and find out what was going on. Hilda quickly concurred. She was still feeling flush from victory and thus generous in mood toward her usually bossy husband.

They had hardly scrambled out of the Morris on squeezing into the pub's crowded car park when a burly man in a bulky white sweater and a hat with a prominent visor that declared his status as a moviemaker suddenly glanced up from a board with a clasp holding a file of papers, bowed, and smiled at them. Taken aback, for smiles in their direction were rare in the village, they nodded in return and moved quickly away. They headed farther down the line of trucks, but when Hilda glanced over her shoulders, she muttered nervously, "He's a followin' on us, Len."

Her spouse took a look. "Leave it to me, my gal. Oi'll take care of 'un if he got some notion against us from them spiteful bastards to the Cornish Arms."

But what the man had to say to them sounded friendly enough. Still, Hilda felt apprehensive and clasped Len nearer to her for support. Their obvious closeness had the man smiling even more broadly.

"Visitors?" he asked. "You wouldn't be from around here, would you?"

Len puffed himself up, more from relief than pride. "Tintagel," he said, "we'm Mr. and Mrs. Len Verran from up to Tintagel."

A sudden change came over the big man. His rather coarse features narrowed and he frowned in the effort of thinking. "You don't say. *Tintagel*, eh? Now that's very, very interesting."

It occurred to both of them that his accent, though faint, was American. It went with the clothes, Hilda thought, and ought to have been accompanied by a large cigar or thick horn-rimmed glasses. "You wouldn' be Canadian, would 'ee?" she asked.

"Me?" came the reply. "Hell, no! Harry Gawthrop is from Liverpool. But Tintagel's the important place right now, and I think I might guess you're from there. We'll be filming in Tintagel when we're through here."

"Oi see," Len said, clearing his throat for further questions.

But Gawthrop hadn't finished. "The series is a multiple one on King Arthur and a whole lot of stuff in all the legends. Now one of those guys was a real little fellow by the name of Frocin. Back in those days they called them dwarfs.

"There's some that still do," Len said, scowling.

Again he was ignored. "This guy—Frocin—was known as the

Dwarf of Tintagel. He was very important. A buddy of Tristan. We reckon he was also a major astrologer. A big guy in a small bod, if you don't mind the joke."

The Verrans said nothing. They sensed there was more to come, and they were right.

"Now we were thinking of leaving this fellow out—tough to cast, if you see what I mean. Christ, it was hard enough to come up with a Merlin, a Sir Galahad, and a Sir Lancelot! But all that's in the bag, including a goddamn Sword Excalibur. After the moor shoot tomorrow, we head for that Dozmary Pool and film that whole section. Then it'll be Tintagel and old Merlin the magician. Got a super bloke for *that* role—bushy beard, long hair, and all. Found him at Waterloo Station. Sleeping under the stars, he was. We've changed the old guy's life, as a matter of fact. Not least the money he's earning. More than he's ever seen before, I'd swear to that!"

The couple stiffened in anticipation.

"The point is, sir, I was wondering whether you'd be at all interested in a screen test? Wouldn't take long and we'd pay you for the trouble of even that." Gawthrop looked away, as if to give the diminutive couple privacy for calculation.

Then Len said something that almost knocked Hilda off her feet. At first she connected it with her surprise victory in the minivan, but she at once dismissed that as fanciful. She repeated his words silently over and over again.

"Oi wouldn' want to do anything like that without Hilda. We're husband and wife, you know. We're a pair. We do things in pairs."

Gawthrop stared at them, then burst into laughter. "Nothing in the script to say no. Then there's no bloody script for this stuff, period! So why not have the Dwarf of Tintagel and His Wife on the payroll? I've read a whole lot of this crap—and believe me, folks, there's one hell of a lot to read!—and I say why not have old Frocin *and* his missus, eh?"

He paused, eyeing them separately. "Mind you, there'd have to be an adjustment over pay. The budget won't run to *two* more character parts than I started out with. And I don't mind telling you guys that we're really thinking budget down here in Cornwall, what with extras in these parts who wouldn't stoop to tie their laces without seeing a quid or more for it!"

Hilda thought it was time to enter the conversation, just in case Len should get huffy or start to defend Pentudy and bow all the way out of the proposition. "Course, we wouldn' want *double* or anything like that, but like the Good Book says, 'The labourer is bravun worthy of his hire'—don' it, you?"

Gawthrop was thinking this odd two would be worth it for their accents alone, even if they hadn't been a couple of precious midgets who had fallen into his hands from heaven! But what he said was: "Of course, they wouldn't be big talking parts. You, Len, would have one speech about 'not weeping for his enemy Tristan' and we'd come up with something for you, ma'am, along the same lines. That would be about it, though we'd make up with the visuals and maybe a voice-over or two." He paused. "By the way, you don't belong to some kind of union, do you?"

Hilda bristled. "Certainly not! We'm estate agents. We got property both to here and to Tintagel."

Gawthrop had some kind of midgets' association in mind, but he wasn't disposed to say so. "Good! Well, the kind of figure I was thinking of was one hundred and thirty-five pounds an hour. Interested?"

While they were shocked into silence at such a princely sum, the TV features director thought he was confronting more Cornish avarice. "That would mean seventy-five percent of the same for you, ma'am. I can't come up with the precise amount now, of course, but I guaranty it'd be enough not to waste your time. I might even squeeze in a couple more lines. Actually, you're lucky. Tintagel will include the wrap-up and by then we should know exactly what's what."

He gave them a wink and they exchanged glances. Winking wasn't part of their alphabet. Len held out his little hand. "P'raps us could sign somethin' in the morning. We'm living to Lanoe. That's the biggest house in Pentudy. You can't mistake of 'un."

And with that that they took their departure—Hilda dying to get back to Lanoe and writing something of the details down for the next day, Len to see if there was anything about a Frocin in Hannah's scant collection of books. Gawthrop was about to head back to the bar of the Cornish Arms, find Helen Gurney, his assistant, and regale her with his exciting news of discovering a delicious couple of Cornish dwarfs who would fit so beautifully into the series. He smiled happily. "Little Cornish nippers" was the label he'd given them, not knowing they were time bombs.

Nine

"Mum, he's not your *brother*, only your cousin!" Quentin not only shouted at his mother, but there were also tears in his eyes.

Alyson knew she'd upset her son, but her chin still jutted obstinately. "In a way, dear, he *is* my brother. In all the important ways he is the only brother I never had. I love him like a brother. That's all that counts."

"Don't we count, Mumsie?"

Hester was ganging up with her brother as usual, Alyson thought. In an odd way she liked that. She certainly preferred to see them united than indulging in those perpetual sibling wrangles that tore her heart. "Of course, you both count. I've never given you call to think otherwise."

"Then why are you thinking of going off and leaving us for him?" Quentin sniffed.

"That's not what I said. The trouble is you children never listen. I'll tell you just once more. Uncle Davey called late last night from

Pentudy, and I could tell in a flash that he wasn't feeling well. I know something's troubling him and that he needs me down there."

As if to give the lie to their earlier reaction, her son persisted with his strenuous objections. "Just because he's hyperneurotic and upset about the old girl's burial and has to invent these stupid dwarf people to grab your attention."

"Mum," her daughter added, "it's all so *obvious*. He resented your not going down there with him right from the start. Now he has to call you in the middle of the night and come up with this crazy story about the Little People trying to cast a spell on him and claiming they date back to King Arthur and all that nonsense."

Alyson wasn't about to be dissuaded from either her evaluation of her cousin's state or her slowly evolving plan to do something about it. "That's just the point, sweetheart! He isn't the kind of person to indulge in fancies like that. Our Davey has his feet firmly on the ground. He was like that—down to earth—right from a little boy. Now my mother was a different story. So was Aunt Hannah, come to that."

But her offspring were as stubborn as she was. "The man is a walking conscience," Hester said. "He only turns up here because he feels he has to. Wouldn't stay, remember? Come to that, he only went down to the bloody funeral because he thought he had to. If you ask me, he detested the old bird."

Quentin wasn't to be outdone by his sibling rival. "If you ask me, he only came over here in the first place because old Ken told him he had to. It's Ken who wears the pants with those two—much as Davey would hate to admit it."

Alyson sighed. She had heard all this so many times before. And it always ended in her tears and the two of them falling over each other to make amends. "Now, if you're finished, I'll tell you what I'd like to happen."

"For him to bugger off back to Canada, that's what I'd like to happen," Quentin said.

His sister decided he was going too far. Sensing her mother's limits, she now backtracked. "What can the Bryant family do for Uncle Davey that would make you happy, Mumsie?"

She was rewarded with the first smile her mother managed to summon since they had come downstairs to join her for elevenses coffee on that Sunday morning. "That's very sweet of you, Hester. What I was thinking was that I should go down there. I just don't think we can do too much from here. Even on the phone I realized he was so involved with what was going on around him that I could have been a thousand miles away. I wouldn't go to where he is in Pentudy, though. At least not right away. I should suggest we meet in Tintagel, rent a car, and drive to the Breakers where my aunt was staying at the end. He kept on about her funeral somehow being phony and that no one from the Breakers was even present. Now you have to agree that was funny, considering she was living there for quite a long time before her death. Only these dwarfs he's fixated on turned up, he says, apart from the minister and the organist. How sad that an old lady of ninety odd can only muster five people at her end and only one of them her own flesh and blood."

"What are we supposed to do?" her son asked sullenly. "If we count at all, that is."

Now Alyson smiled at him. "I was just coming to that, darling. The Breakers business should only take a day or so. Then I'd love you two to come down and we'd all go over to Lanoe House. After all, you'll be the only inheritors of the place after I've gone. Davey and I talked about that some time ago, and he agrees totally. These Little People Davey mentions think they have some claim, but it's absolute nonsense. The instructions in Aunt Nora's will were quite clear. Her portion was to go to Hannah, provided it all ultimately be left to Davey and me and our descendants, if there were such. There was absolutely no one else as potential beneficiaries. And then, I was thinking, we could have a little holiday. I could show you Grandpa Bryant's house in St. Keverne, and I should suggest you bring your snorkelling gear, Quentin. The weather can still be very nice there in the autumn. In any case, you could both wear those new wetsuits you used this past summer."

"You don't have to *bribe* us, Mum," Hester said. "We're not that bad, are we?"

Her mother shook her jowelled head with great seriousness. "What I'm asking is that my darling children come down to Cornwall to help me. To back me up if these people continue with their preposterous claim to the old Bryant Dower house. Just your presence, you see, would double the strength of our position. We could then have a powwow. Who knows? If we find that Davey has been exaggerating a little, then we might suggest this couple stay on as caretakers for a while. But I think these things need on-the-spot decisions. Now can I rely on the two most important people in the world to help me?"

"Well, if you put it like that..." Quentin trailed off, his meaning clear, even if he was reluctant to spell out anything vaguely tantamount to an apology.

Hester was more forthright. "We'll be there, Mummy," she said, using a term for her mother that was reserved for special occasions. "I can take time off at school. I never have and the other kids do it all the time. Same for you, Quent?"

Her brother nodded. "Can I bring Nigel, Mum? He could do with an introduction to the country. He's getting far too decadent in the city. Besides, there's no one to look after him if we all go away."

Alyson wasn't altogether happy about the clumber spaniel accompanying them to Cornwall, but she didn't want any more of Quentin's opposition that morning. "Of course, darling. He'll be company for you. Just because I need you there for a specific purpose doesn't mean you children shouldn't enjoy yourselves with a little break from routine."

But when shortly after son and daughter trooped upstairs again, Alyson was left with a sense of everything not being quite as neatly determined and satisfactory as she would have hoped. The dog was one thing, but she soon dismissed that. Alyson was used to bowing to the inevitable, or just the threat of further acrimony if her second son's will was thwarted. It wasn't only that he was her Benjamin, but always, hovering there, was the painful presence of the absent Allen incarcerated in St. Bride's whose sore mind was in no position to be either denied or placated.

After a while her thoughts returned from her children to Davey and that ominous phone call. She had been as honest with Quentin and Hester as she could, but there were other factors she not only thought beyond the scope of their young minds but also were so disturbing to her personally that she found difficulty in formulating them for herself. It was to do not only with Davey but his second cousin, her eldest son. It had never occurred to her before—not once she now fiercely insisted to herself—but somehow last night, when Davey was rattling on about the Verrans from Tintagel, she suddenly, shockingly, had an image of her son in St. Bride's shouting and screaming at her that she didn't understand the demons pursuing him. Sitting there now, she remembered precisely when Davey had evoked that image. It was when he was loudly insisting that he knew for certain the Verrans were of another time, had been manifest earlier as the evil Dwarf Frocin.

She also recalled something else. She had told her children what a stolid little boy Davey had been. But it hadn't always been so. There had been that incident on top of Jubilee Rock involving her parents when they had taken her up to North Cornwall to see the relatives. Davey couldn't have been much more than thirteen at the time. There had been an incident with an adder or viper. They were having a picnic lunch there. Her Uncle Wesley saw the serpent first, curled under a frond of bracken, its zigzag markings standing out prominently and suggesting, her uncle said afterward, that it had recently shed its skin. Perhaps it was that which made the reptile aggressive. In any case, just as Davey, walking in front of his father, was about to pass it, the creature rose from its coil, tongue flickering and V-marked head swaying as if about to strike.

Alyson had never seen Uncle Wesley move faster—before or since the incident. But just as his son turned, saw the adder, and raised his bare arm, not so much to move it from harm's way but incredibly—it seemed to the little girl—to stroke the animal's flat head as he splayed fingers and moved his hand nearer. But before there could be any interpretation of Davey's action, his father had grabbed a granite stone from the surface of the giant rock and started to pound it again and again on the coiled shape.

Soon there was no more coiling or uncoiling but an increasingly bloody mess in the gravelly dust of the boulder's surface: crushed bracken leaves, bespattered with the victim's entrails, an almost decapitated head with the eyes bulging from the force of the rock thudding repeatedly against it.

But it wasn't the horror of that which so caught Alyson up in fear. It was the violent reaction of her cousin. He was screaming at his father. "Don't! Don't do that! You're horrible! It's just a little snake. What has it done to you? I hate you! You're an evil bully and God should kill you." He went on and on, but she couldn't remember all of it, just her uncle seeking to pacify the demented youngster as he jumped up and down in rage.

"It was about to strike you, Davey," his father said. "It's an adder, son. They're poisonous. They can kill you. It was you or him and I'm your dad."

By this time Davey's fit was drowning in tears. His shouts were less loud and his words slowed down. "It was one of God's babies…we have no right…God made Cornwall a refuge for the poor snakes fleeing Ireland." He muttered something about St. Patrick, but it was incoherent; besides, his voice had now degenerated into a hoarse whisper.

Alyson shifted in her seat. Of course, on the phone there was no reference to adders or, for that matter, wild creatures. But it wasn't the image wrought by his actual words but the sound from his throat that had brought back that ancient memory. He had sounded, well, if not hysterical, at least totally refusing of opposition. He also seemed somehow stuck in the past. She distinctly remembered that atop Jubilee Rock he had mentioned St. Patrick. This time it had been King Arthur, Tintagel and, of course, the two dwarfs who seemed to obsess him. She wondered if there was any connection between the two, then shook her head when it all seemed so fanciful, so extravagant.

But when she forced herself away from all such comparisons, her tired mind went back to her unhappy son and his mental plight. She recalled reading somewhere that the Cornish were more subject to such conditions than other people. Perhaps there was some horrible link between her Allen and Davey—two ends of a generational scale, as it were.

Then she shook herself violently, the whole bulk of her body, before getting up and crossing to the phone. That kind of thought was getting her nowhere, simply depressing her more and more. Punching out the number for the railway to establish both an itinerary and a convenient schedule, she sagged with relief when a voice answered and she was back in the world of the prosaic where she was safely at home.

TEN

Several things had been happening to Davey for which he would have been hard put to apply the term *rational*. One was, knowing he might well bump into the Verrans, why he decided to revisit Lanoe House on his own. Was it with the vague hope of discovering something about Hannah that his time there with the dwarfs had signally failed to do?

In any case, it was while he was there on this second occasion that he had the first of a series of odd experiences that determined his life over the next few days. He had made his way into his Aunt Nora's special room. In fact, she had utilized several rooms in the house, but this was the one his Aunt Hannah called her *lair*. He wasn't even sure why he had chosen that as a place to sit, but he did know as soon as he had and was facing the few shelves of books—the nearest approach to a library in the whole house—that he felt he was in the right place.

Maybe he'd seen too many movies—the old brand, that is, with a leisurely story, domestic drama, and both people and their accommodations suggesting power and opulence. But he sensed immediately there was something over by the books that awaited him, something to do with Aunt Nora rather than the more familiar Hannah. So powerful was this sensation that he had barely sat before rising again and crossing to the shelves. The bulk of the books were popular paperbacks. His eyes scarcely scanned them but roved instead toward the six or seven scattered hardback volumes stacked at each end. He grimaced sourly. They were obviously serving the lowly purpose of bookends for the pop stuff sandwiched between them. These books included an encyclopedia, a dictionary, and *Cruden's Unabridged Concordance of the Bible*. He thought the presence of the last odd in that it should surely have been in Bible-quoting Hannah's collection, wherever that was deposited, and he considered it highly unlikely the two women had shared their books.

It was this notion that determined he take the dark blue tome down to see if a name was inscribed inside. Even as he saw that of Nora Bryant neatly written on the flypaper, a folded square of paper slipped out and fluttered to the ground. He was so surprised he didn't immediately stoop to reclaim it. Davey was thinking that scarcely twenty-four hours had elapsed since he was himself feigning to get such a thing to happen in order to dupe the rapacious Verrans and set them off on a wild-goose chase.

It seemed too much for a coincidence. Davey looked around Nora's dimly lit room, taking in the heavy horsehair sofa with its ornate Victorian squirls in the mahogany wood. He remembered how escaping strands of horsehair had pricked his thighs when, as a child, he had sat obediently in his short pants and listened to his aunt lecturing him on the problems of being a wicked little boy.

Davey had to open the two folded sheets very carefully. Brown from oxidization and consequently brittle, they were also undated, but because of their frail condition he ascribed them to a relatively distant past. There was no preamble, and the writing, in an agitated hand, wobbled across the unlined pages.

They call you Hannah, but that means "God has favoured me," and I of all people know that to be untrue. You bear the name of the Prophet Samuel's mother, yet you are the *mother* of nothing save denial. You denied your husband. You denied your Jewish origins. And, how in your infinite cruelty, you have denied me!

I have protected you, poured out my heart for you, ever since you first came under our roof. But you rejected me as you rejected your religion and your duties as my brother's wife. You will probably never see this—at least in my lifetime. Perhaps that is as it should be. Meant just for my eyes. I who so long ago gave up my Redeemer when I abandoned my presence at Holy Mass where I used to lovingly offer up prayers for your soul every time I knelt at the Altar.

That was when I turned to the moor, that place of wild spirits where I didn't feel forever under God's Judgement and condemned for my love for you which you only ever spurned . But you followed me out there, didn't you? You used the excuse of that darling creature I gave you on your birthday and which you cruelly twisted against me.

Perhaps it was Satan who brought you to Cornwall to seduce me. A beautiful Jewess—oh, God, you were beautiful!—intent on destroying this weak Christian through her perversity. A perversity I fought so hard all my life until you came to Lanoe on the arms of my beloved brother. I was so helpless. I could prevent the world invading me from Pentudy. But not when it had been invited into this very house, insisted we be called sisters, and forcing domestic intimacies between us. The very closeness of you! Oh, Hannah, that I could not fight.

But how I have paid for it! You refused my love, despised its very nature. But I cannot hate you. I cannot even keep my distance from you. When I want to be angry at you, I can only weep for a Hannah who utterly ignores me. That is why I spew these words. I hate myself for what I am. I am never free from anger. You and your demons have truly made me *the unhappiest woman in Cornwall*.

Davey folded the two sheets carefully back into their matching creases. But instead of reinserting them into the biblical concordance, he crushed them into a thousand tiny fragments, fiercely rubbing them between his palms. Then he took the mess over to the sash window and fumbled with a couple of fingers to unleash the lock and create an opening. Then he let his aunt's anguish waft out onto the night air. He vaguely hoped it would be caught by the wind and taken as dust to the rocks and tarns of the moor. At that stark moment he knew a spasm of relief that none but himself would now read his blood aunt's words. For a moment he stood there, staring but unseeing in her crumpled wake, allowing the cold wind to play over him. He felt a Bryant in a Bryant's house, securing a secret of their clan. It was the first time since coming home that he was secure in a role, but the satisfaction was fleeting.

Only then did he allow himself to rock in the immense knowledge that he hadn't been the first gay entity in their family living in such isolation and self-absorption up there on the lip of the moor. He sat down abruptly at the impact of that. It was akin to an attack of vertigo. His mind pursed the implications. If all this was a matter of inheritance, then maybe that second cousin of his, young Quentin, was indeed cut from the same cloth. Perhaps it was this, too, that had provided the sharp-edged tension he had invariably sensed lay somewhere deep if never entirely dormant in Hannah's attitude toward him. She had hated the same in him as in her Sapphic sister-in-law.

He heard a sound from downstairs and at once thought it might be the Verrans. What if they suspected his genetic inheritance from one aunt as they feared the material one from the other? Davey was suddenly glad he had urged Alyson to come and join him. He knew one way or another he could draw on her love for him and use it as social camouflage before the perpetually suspicious Verrans.

But his thinking also made him realize how much more now he was reluctant to encounter them when they returned from their trip to Penzance. And equally, how inopportune such an encounter would be in that very house where it now appeared as an innocent he had stirred the hostility of a man-hating woman and another who insisted on seeing him as Nora's ally.

As it happened, his wish was to be partially granted. The Verrans were to beard him in the Cornish Arms the very next morning—where, after a restless night, troubled not only by dreams but by the noisy talk from the film crew inhabiting the neighbouring rooms, he was about to head for St. Keverne and the hoped for solace of parental graves.

ELEVEN

If Davey hadn't begun the day by feeling so undone, so "apart at the seams," as he used to describe himself to Ken after a bibulous or tense evening back in Vancouver in the old days when he returned frazzled from the newspaper, he might have appreciated the elements of farce that attended his encounter with Len Verran as they met in the small village square of which the Cornish Arms and its outbuildings formed the eastern flank. Although the little man hardly extended his arm in greeting, he did vouchsafe a cocky smile. And Davey thought the fellow was even more insufferably jaunty than when he last beheld him.

"Bravun morning, Mr. Bryant. You'm still wid us then?"

"Yes, of course, Mr. Verran. Haven't finished my investigations yet." Davey was about to embark upon an elaborate scheme of detection that he decided would, for Len Verran's sake, centre on the unknown specifics of Hannah's last days at Lanoe, which the Verrans had presumably shared with her before carting her off to the Breakers. This, he hoped, would put a bolt of fear up the diminutive backsides of both Len and his spouse as he was about to hint at arcane deeds and his suspicions of their possible involvement.

But before he could even get started the bluff figure of Harry Gawthrop, the TV director, materialized on the doorsteps of the village inn. He addressed Len but not under that name. "So how is our Frocin of Tintagel?" he asked. "And Sister Frocin, too?"

Len nodded with satisfaction, but Davey came close to swooning. The Canadian was even more shattered when the little man called back, "We'm thrivin', maister. And both anxious to get to Tintagel wid 'ee and show 'ee our friend Merlin and Tristan, too." Len had spent part of the night back at Lanoe reading a popularized version of Sir Thomas Malory's *Le Morte D'Arthur* which, according to the flyleaf inscription, belonged to Father Trewin when, as vicar of Pentudy, he had lent it to the Bryants and which had obviously never been returned. Fortified by his scanning of that work, Len was able to embroider further. "The Dwarfs o' Tintagel will introduce 'ee to Galahad, Guinevere, an' a whole lot more! We'll keep your TV filmmakers busy!"

"I have to leave Frocin with his friends," Davey muttered, and almost ran around the corner to the car park and his rented Rover. How to describe his state of mind as he roared the vehicle through the village, splashing across the ford where he had encountered Joseph William Clemo, the itinerant knife grinder, heading grimly for the maze of lanes that lay beyond? In fact, his thoughts were a blur, a hodgepodge of amazement at having his suspicions about the Verrans so dramatically confirmed by the burly filmmaker—that the arrogant little man was indeed an updated version of the legendary Frocin, the Dwarf of Tintagel. That he and his sister dwarf were in collusion against him, determined to rid him from their realm and ready, he didn't doubt, to exploit the unhappy rift between his aunts, imprisoned in Lanoe. For that matter, who knew if the Frocins—as he was beginning to call them—hadn't inserted that terrible outpouring from Nora expressly for his eyes to feed on? Perhaps they had invented the knife grinder to lead him down false paths with his talk about the warring women and Hannah's wanton behaviour with her parish priest.

Just as the vicarage hove into sight, Davey saw the gaunt cleric who had informed him that Hannah was a foundling. On this second occasion, though, the priest was dressed somewhat differently. Father Hector Laws-Johnston was still clad in a soutane as he sailed down the narrow sidewalk of the village street, but his head was crowned with a large-brimmed clerical hat of a kind Davey had only seen on rural French curés and that mainly in movies. His head bowed, he held a breviary up before moving lips, but didn't see the Rover as it approached.

Davey was still in a jumbled world of medieval Cornwall and late-nineteenth-century England, of baleful enemies and loved-soured relatives. It suddenly occurred to him that the priest might liberate him from these confusing pressures, so he slowed the car to a halt and opened the window. "Good morning, Father. Can you tell me something? Did you know my Aunt Hannah was Jewish?"

The priest stopped muttering his prayers and lifted his head so that Davey could now see his lined and pallid face. "Could be…could be. Stoke Newington had many Jews at that time." He wrinkled his features into what was presumably intended as a smile. "They were all so very poor. It isn't hard to imagine the impoverished mother of a little girl leaving her off at the parish church in the hope that someone would adopt her. We remember the story of Moses in Exodus, don't we? Of the baby Moses being left in a basket amid the reeds of the Nile in the hope that someone kindly disposed would discover him?"

Davey was desperately trying to recall the biblical passage when the old man tipped his preposterously large hat, politely inclined his head, and moved on again, his lips once more responding to his reopened breviary. Mercifully the Canadian had then to concentrate on the bewildering curves of the lanes lacing Pentudy and St. Keverne rather than dwell on the priest's reply to his question. Although it was now the fullness of autumn, the leaves stubbornly clung to the blackthorn and alder of the hedgerows so that it was still gloomy until he emerged into open meadow just prior to drawing up at the granite war memorial erected outside the graveyard that stood as a stony apron surrounding the parish church.

For the first time since reading Nora's lament, Davey felt less weighed down with doubts and omens as he confidently wound his way along the gravel path to his father's grave. Standing there confronting the already lichen-stained slate, he was mildly aware that no breeze blew across his bared head. Then this was St. Keverne, deep in the elm-clad Amble Valley, and not Pentudy where the wind blew endlessly off the moor.

For the umpteenth occasion—for he visited this grave every time he came back to Cornwall—he read the words: WESLEY DAVID BRYANT: BORN 1870. DIED 1964. His father's name and details were directly under those of his dad's mother, for they were buried in the same spot, just as his mother was buried in her own father's grave higher in the churchyard. He wondered fleetingly if it were a Polkinghorne—his mother's maiden name—or Bryant idiosyncrasy to be buried with a parent rather than a spouse, or a Cornish or Celtic practice. Anyway, there it was—Daddy resting eternally with *his* mama; Mummy with her beloved poppa. Each generation, he ruminated, providing a period-scented term for its parents.

As he stood listening to the tinkle of invisible water from the Amble River—really just a stream—and the cheerful call of jackdaws nesting in the Norman church tower, he pondered the duality of his usually shy and gentle father transformed by superstition into a man fearful of jackdaws, made paranoid by their reputation of a roguish propensity to steal, equally apprehensive of magpies as omens of death and illegitimate offspring if seen in numbers, and his atavistic, Bible-spurred horror of serpents as the source of all evil (highlighted, as Davey once more recalled, when witnessing as a child his usually mild father pounding the adder on Jubilee Rock to death before the boy's horrified eyes). In quick compensation, though, the son invoked the memory of a snow-haired, buxom mother who wore a smile he rarely recalled being switched off.

Davey eased his weight from one foot to the other. He, still the biped, felt grimy before his father's recumbent form. Wesley Bryant had always been so much more innocent than his son. Davey thought it significant that neither his dad nor his uncle had indulged in foxhunting or even riding for pleasure as their cousins had. Both had returned home after 1918, full of guilt for man's obscene treatment of his equine companions on the battlefronts of Europe. The Violets, Princes, and Rubies of the North Cornwall farms were made to do their cart-horse duties, but with great gentleness before being rubbed down and released for quiet evenings of munching, farting, and rolling on their giant backs with feathered legs stuck out puppy-like above the rabbit-nibbled turf. Their owners, at least the two Bryant brothers, thinking as they turned lush Cornish pasture into rich loam at plough time, thinking sadly of the shell-denuded soil of the Western Front perforated with the countless equine corpses, legs stiff to the sullied sky.

Up to that point his parental past had succeeded in keeping the present at bay. Then he reflected on his inherited genes from this so different man buried there, and his thoughts flew back to Nora and that dreadful testimony. At once made restless over the possible legacy of the Bryants, he made himself think of the Polkinghornes and his mother, wondering if it was their clan that was responsible for his difference from his dad. It was enough to propel him up the steep slope of scattered graves to where his mother lay parallel with Poppa Lester Polkinghorne, a grandfather who had departed Cornwall before he had even arrived!

He didn't linger long at the second gravesite. The thoughts now insistently winging his way made it too unsettling. Instead he returned to the Rover, giving thought, however, to the fact that he had rented the vehicle specifically because it had been his daddy's brand of car in which he had learned to drive as a teenager.

But the coincidence of cars proved weak as consolation and of short duration. He debated phoning Ken and discussing everything with him. But in the end he decided on a carefully worded letter. Ken's lawyer mind was too sharp, too precise, and was unlikely to prevaricate comfortably in areas that remained shady and unproven. The question of Nora's sad testament was a case in point. Davey knew very well that Ken would want a most detailed explanation before allowing himself any conclusion. As he drove the final leg of the four-mile trip between the villages, Davey realized with a lowering of spirits that in no part of her narrative did Nora specifically refer to her sexual predilections. And, to make matters worse, he had now destroyed whatever evidence that might have suggested otherwise.

When he got back to Pentudy, he parked away from where the TV vehicles stood, choosing a deserted lane behind the inn. He passed through the slate-porched front door of the wisteria-covered building surreptitiously and crept up to his tiny room with its rough-hewn oak beams to compose a careful letter he wanted to send as quickly as possible to his lover. In the end, though, he felt so dithery and uncertain that after composing the letter and sealing it he decided to back it up with a phone call.

TWELVE

en Verran rolled up his little sleeping bag, preparatory to taking it out of Lanoe along with that of his wife, and stuffed them into the trunk of their Morris. They had decided to camp there in the two bedrooms no longer. For one thing, they'd received not a single reply from any of their advertisements in such magazines as *Country Life* and the *Come to Cornwall* guides, and that was even before they'd managed to exile Hannah to the Breakers.

Their plan, however, was vaguely conceived and somewhat bereft of details. The fact was they were far from unanimous over it all, one wanting to dispose of the building as either an elegant bed-and-breakfast or guest house, the other wishing to sell it as a small retirement home for no more than four or five people. Len had favoured the former and had even toyed with the idea of running it as a mildly posh restaurant that specialized in Cornish cuisine. But Hilda had pooh-poohed that idea from the outset, claiming Pentudy was far too remote and unheard of to attract the kind of well-heeled diner her husband had in mind. On the other hand, he had fiercely countered her alternative suggestion that they should rent—if they failed to make an outright sale—the property to a small group of the elderly or ailing in that godforsaken moorland spot for no other reason than the gales and alternating fog and rain would play havoc with both the rheumatic and the arthritic, those being the only category of elderly English, he insisted, who were disposed to regard even that part of Cornwall as a geriatric ward.

The advent of Davey Bryant at the funeral had been a rude surprise and a discouragement. They were both convinced that Hannah was thoroughly grateful for their ministrations and persuaded by them that she should eventually enter the Breakers outside Tintagel. The old lady had also hinted frequently that she would like them to take over the house. The only snag was they were only too aware that no will had ever materialized.

In spite of their incessant efforts to convince the newcomer that their occupancy and ownership of Lanoe had been Hannah's dying wish, Hilda, the realistic one, was certain that if things came to a court case, they were unlikely to be the victors. Her pessimism was compounded by the fact that the Canadian had strongly hinted that the woman in London had papers somewhere to prove that Lanoe House belonged to her and the visiting Davey. All the more relief then at the arrival of Harry Gawthrop and the unexpected offer of lucrative TV roles for the two of them.

As soon as Len had loaded the sleeping bags, toiletries, and the small number of domestic possessions they'd brought from home into the Morris, they would be off once more to their native Tintagel to take up their Frocin characters and to attend the local library to collect far more details of the successors to the medieval dwarfs they had been chosen to play.

Len was already getting into the rhythm of things, while his spouse remained more equivocal, insisting almost hourly to him that she required documentary evidence of the BBC's intentions toward them. She never tired of pointing out that they'd seen nothing like a contract yet and that when she'd vaguely mentioned "residuals" to Gawthrop, he'd replied in even vaguer terms about all that being outside his domain but that he'd duly take it up with the relevant parties.

By this time Len was anxious to pursue his research—a wholly new activity for him—and from the little he'd already digested the previous night, the Little People loomed in far greater importance and respect than he'd ever dreamed of. At least in that far-off Celtic and Cornish world of King Arthur's time, according to the pages of the unreturned book from the vicarage and the two home encyclopedias he'd unearthed and which he learned from their inscriptions belonged to the two female inhabitants who had probably used them as sources of verbal ammunition in their incessant wars over every subject under the sun. Then, Len mused, while those two Bryants were doing their fighting their distant Verran cousins had been equally wasting their time by busily underplaying their shortness of stature and striving to negate or deflect the mockery and ridicule they were convinced followed in their wake wherever they went among their own malicious Cornish.

Even so, driving back to their "villa" from Pentudy, the couple cautiously avoided any discussion about the sudden financial potential arising directly from their limited stature. Instead they concentrated on safer topics holding less likelihood of disagreement. It was Hilda who guided the conversation.

"Know what, Len? Oi do reckon we should pay a little visit to the Breakers again. Find out if the ole girl left anything with they people there. Everything were so rushed last toime."

Len, who as usual was at the wheel when the two were driving together, scowled. "Bloody hostile, too, if 'ee asks me! That bitch what runs the plaice, instead o' being grateful to us for bringin' more business, scarce give us the toime o' day! Anyways, Hilda, all that can wait. We got more important things to do—what with our filmmakin'. That Gawthrop told Oi we was gin be bravun busy, even before they cameras get rollin'. They b'aint *that* small roles, whatever you keep suggestin'."

She changed the subject. "Oi do wonder what mischief that Canadian will get up to when we b'aint there. Oi don' trust him no more than you do, Len."

But her husband wasn't about to be placated. "No more you should! Slippery bastard wi' that sarky tongue, jest loike Oi told of 'ee roight off the bat!"

Hilda returned to her earlier notion. "When we *do* get toime to go there—to the Breakers, that is—Oi reckon we should talk to that ole woman what was so close to Hannah. The one that had nothin' to say last toime?"

Len pressed his little foot hard on the accelerator. "When will 'ee understand, woman? That koind b'aint gin talk to the loikes on us at *any* toime. For one thing, the ole hag were nothin' but a bloody snob. Did 'ee hark on her snooty accent? To her we was nothing but Cornish peasants." He was silent for a moment, then added, "Cornish *dwarf* peasants, that is."

Hilda thought of a placatory response but decided not to. While Len was in that snarky mood, she knew from long experience it wasn't worth it. For the rest of the journey home they hardly spoke.

THIRTEEN

Alyson's broad features lit up as she saw her cousin waiting for her at the end of the railway platform. Even from that distance she thought he wore a hunted look, and that made her want to clasp and comfort him. On the way down from London, when she had to dismount from the express train at Exeter and take a slower affair consisting of only three cars on a branch line to Okehampton where he was to collect her, there had been a dramatic turnabout in the weather that had distinctly affected her. The heavy grey skies that had accompanied her from the moment she had bid two disconsolate children goodbye and trudged toward the tube station—she dutifully refused to take taxis for such a brief distance—suddenly fell away and from the carriage window she stared out on brilliant blue and an unencumbered sun.

She could feel the unseasonable warmth through the plate-glass window and that encouraged her, pushing away the sea of doubts and misgivings that invariably swam in her head and had received extra impetus following her decision to join her cousin at such short notice and, as her children were never tired of reiterating, such paucity of evidence as to his true state of being.

The sight of Davey was further fillip to her spirits. Abandoning her small suitcase on the platform and holding on to a wide-brimmed felt hat, she scampered her rather ungainly girth toward her cousin. By the time she reached him, he had responded to her wreath of smiles and held his arms outstretched in welcome. A stranger would have interpreted the tableau as her feet actually left the ground as a loving couple who had been separated for an undue length of time. People at the ticket gate smiled, two children nudged each other. Davey and Alyson were impervious.

When Davey had collected her bag and they approached his Rover, he spoke coherently for the first time since her arrival. "I'm glad you could make it, Alyson. I wasn't sure you could arrange things with the kids and that."

She was still beaming. "Oh, they couldn't have been more cooperative. In fact, I hope they'll be joining us in a day or so."

He let that go. "As a special treat, Al," he said, using a term he hadn't invoked for her in years, "I thought I'd drive you back to Pentudy over the moors. It's a perfect day to see them, don't you think? They've been the best thing about my coming down for the funeral. As for the rest, well, I told you things on the phone, but there's more than that."

She squeezed his hand impulsively. It was now her turn to leave certain topics for later. "Is there anything specially you want to show me on the moor? I always felt they marked some of the happiest times of my childhood when we came up from Falmouth. But, of course, they meant so much more to you—living right on the edge of them."

"It's about all of Cornwall that's left for us to recognize," he grumbled. "And even so they've been nibbling away at that."

She was about to remind him that she thought the authorities had elevated the moors to some kind of national park—or was that only Dartmoor in Devon? Once more she determined to act with the utmost discretion. She had already noticed a slight twitch to his temples, which was unfamiliar, and she couldn't be sure it was only her imagination that perceived an odd glint in his eyes.

In fact, the route Davey chose after leaving Launceston was to remain on the A-30 until the village of Bolventor when he took time out to make a left turn and visit the mile-round Dozmary Pool where the knight, Sir Galahad, was reputed to have flung King Arthur's Excalibur, never to be seen again. But what Davey was remembering was the family visit with the Falmouth Bryants and his Uncle Joseph, half in play, half seriously, "baptizing" him in the cold grey waters of the small lake with the names of Davey Arthur on behalf of the Cornish Gorsedd to which his father had recently been elected a bard. Davey had felt very proud though uncertain of what was going on. Alyson had cried.

"Oh, Davey!" she now exclaimed. "It hasn't changed one little bit!"

Even as she spoke there was a disturbance along the track down which they had just bumped. There, in caravan-style, were the three large white vehicles that constituted the King Arthur Legend unit of the BBC.

Davey grimaced. "It'll change now. Next time you come here expect a huge car park. Come on, let's go."

In the Rover, going back to the highway and the village of Bolventor before heading north again to Alternun and taking the snaking lanes toward the coast, he told her about the movie project. "They've apparently woven dozens of Arthurian legends into one package that will end up in weeks and weeks of installments and which will obviously drag tourists down here next summer by the hundreds of thousands." And when she didn't seem to stir adequately in depression at that black thought, he added, "And don't think they haven't done their homework! It is the BBC, after all, and they even researched in Tintagel and dug up the fact that those awful Verrans who are trying to steal Aunt Hannah's house from us are direct descendants of that evil Frocin who in the Middle Ages was the enemy of Tristan."

Alyson savoured all this. It was quite obvious that her cousin's voice was getting more heated. She had expected the subject of the dwarfs to come up, but the BBC and the filmmaking was a surprise. "Could they have absolute proof, darling? I mean, the Verrans and this Frocin person, it was all so very long ago, and you did say it was all legend, didn't you?"

Davey shrugged. "Have you forgotten so quickly? Legend? History? This is Cornwall—what's the difference? What's more, this is Bodmin Moor. Look ahead of you, over there toward Brown Willy. I doubt if that view has changed much since the Bronze Age!"

Alyson saw her opportunity to get him off the dwarfs. "I love it! As a child, it was coming up here to the moors from Falmouth and meeting the rest of you that was the highlight of my holidays. Remember the picnics on Jubilee Rock?" She hoped he didn't remember the adder....

It seemed not. "Do you know that until I came down this time and started to dig up things about the moor, such as why it meant so much to Aunt Hannah and Aunt Nora, I had no idea why the Rock was called that. I thought the Jubilee was that of King George V in 1935 when I was a kid. Not a bit of it. It was named to celebrate the Golden Jubilee of King George *III* back in 1810. Then, up here, what's the difference of a century or two?"

The heather was in fullest bloom at that time of year. Davey lowered his window and slowed the car. "Listen!" he commanded.

They heard a muffled roar like a giant snoring. She stared out at the sun-shot scene that caused boulders to dance in the heat haze and the flaming gorse to shimmer. "What is it?" she whispered, truly awestruck.

"The bees," he explained. "The heather brings them from all over. Don't you remember Aunt Hannah's honey?"

She nodded, though she didn't. "I'm sure where you live now,

Davey, there are fantastic landscapes, marvellous views. But surely in the world there's nothing *more* beautiful than all this." She waved her plump arm in invitation.

He smiled fondly at his cousin, welcoming her words. Together they quite forgot the capricious moods of the moor, the snarl of Atlantic wind, and the sudden descent of the obliterating mists across the treacherous bogs. Perhaps such factors lurked in the wings of his mind, because he suddenly revved the engine and they moved much faster toward Pentudy, the Cornish Arms, and their concomitant distractions.

FOURTEEN

T o say that the landlord of the Cornish Arms was surprised when Davey Bryant returned with Alyson in tow would be to put it mildly. Then Jack Pascoe had started with a whole bunch of suppositions about the man inhabiting room nine that had proved wrong. Among these was the publican's conviction that his guest was an American—or "Yank," as he was wont to say. This was partly to do with the fact that Pascoe was of a second-generation Pentudy family and liked to think that as head of the "communications center," which was how he regarded the village inn, he knew everyone for miles around, as well as their histories and scandals. He didn't know Davey, although he was well versed in the immediate Bryant family and, of course, the late inhabitants of Lanoe.

This unfamiliarity irritated the landlord, especially when his transatlantic guest leaned confidentially over the bar the very first night of his stay and remarked that Pascoe's Uncle Tom had worked for Davey's father in St. Keverne as a boy fresh from school aged fourteen and had once cried from the rawness of his hands when sent during his first week of employment by the Bryants to uproot tough dock plants in a soured field. Davey also told the landlord how much his family had appreciated receiving each autumn a shoe box of figs from the southern wall of the pub's garden. Both his mother and the two childless women of Lanoe would then stuff the ripe figs with clotted cream and serve them for dessert, Davey informed the landlord.

But the publican didn't appreciate Davey's expressed gratitude for these childhood recollections of such a delicacy. From then on every effort of Davey to cement his relationship with the moorland village through Pascoe met with a Cornish annoyance at foreigners— derisively called *emmets* behind their backs, a word that also meant *ants*—and a resentment on the landlord's part at this newcomer with his lofty claims, in spite of his transatlantic accent, of being a patriotic local at odds with such outsiders as the interloping Verrans from Tintagel. Hilda and Len happened to have quickly become two good customers of the Cornish Arms since their arrival at Lanoe the previous year.

It wasn't surprising then that Pascoe found Alyson Bryant to be of considerable interest. In fact, he could hardly wait to get this new guest on her own. The private lounge—reserved exclusively for those staying at the inn—was one of the oldest parts of the seventeenth-century pub. It was also among the most ill-lit. That was because it boasted a single window, which consisted of small leaded squares of some antiquity, but which was again partially obscured by the large splayed leaves of the ancient fig tree that grew immediately beyond it and which had provided Davey with such fond gustatory memories as well as having given the inn a reputation throughout the region. The room also boasted the rather uneven and bumpy walls indicating the ubiquitous Cornish building material known as cob (a mixture of slate and clay), but in this case it was so heavily papered and coarsely painted over that it looked as if had been constructed from leftovers from the granite boulders of the moor itself.

The heavy rusticity was further complemented by rough rafters across the low ceiling. Some benighted instinct for rural elegance had concealed their veritable age and charm with thick black paint, an echo of several of the small guest rooms at the top of the inn that were adorned with the same funereal shade. Neither interior nor exterior decoration was a Cornish forte.

The landlord quickly took his chance when he glimpsed Davey walking toward the car park. "Your first visit to these parts then, Mrs. Bolitho? You'm from up to London, Oi gather."

Alyson was nursing a half-pint tankard of cider at the corner table where Davey had left her, telling her to stay put until his return. She felt greatly daring to be sitting there, the only woman. "Falmouth originally," she volunteered. "But London for the last little while." She suddenly thought of the two free-spirited children left at home, her darling firstborn, Allen, so long a prisoner of his own stricken mind, as well as physically incarcerated in St. Bride's, and was amazed she could contract such life-shaping factors into "little while."

She smiled up toward the bar, though. She wasn't about to elaborate on all that before strangers. Alyson prided herself on being a private person, and neither publicans, a profession quite unknown to her, nor hairdressers, whose kind she visited weekly, were of a social category about to persuade her to divulge personal matters.

Or so she assumed. Then she had never met the likes of Jack Pascoe, who had spent so much of his life developing his considerable wiles to ferret details, personal or otherwise, from his daily patrons. "You and Mr. Bryant, you'm brother and sister then? That's very nice. Oi'm very close to me sister, too."

"Oh, no," she corrected quickly. "We're cousins. *First* cousins, that is. I come from the Falmouth side of the family. Mr. Bryant's from up here, of course. St. Keverne?"

"Oh, that's it, is it? Well, Oi gather you'm pretty close and that.

From what he was saying, that is."

Alyson was pleased by what she heard. She relaxed a little more. "I'm an only child as he is. In a way, we're sort of honorary siblings. That's what I tell my children."

"Got kiddies then?"

"Three," she said, closing her lips firmly. Her babies, she was thinking, were of the world she'd temporarily left. This one was just to do with her and Davey—at least as far as this man was concerned.

Not at all discouraged, Pascoe decided to try another tack. "Course, we was all put out to hear of your aunt's passin' away. She were your aunt, weren' she—up to Lanoe House?"

This time Alyson nodded, sipped her cider, and waited for him to go on.

"Oi understand the ole lady was up to visitin' your cousin, out there to America from toime to toime. Well, for a while, that was, when Oi do reckon all that travellin' got too much for her. She didn' come in here very often, you moight say. But Oi'd bump into her out there in the square once in a while. Reckon her memory was failin', poor lady. Oi bide Oi never heard about where her was goin' and who her was visitin' in them foreign parts."

Alyson straightened in her chair. "Well, her nephew, of course. He and his friend made a great deal of fuss about her. She was always made so welcome. She just loved visiting them in Vancouver," she informed him. Then as afterthought and remembering Davey's so oft-repeated words, she added, "Canada, that is. Vancouver, British Columbia, Canada."

"Ah, yes, his *friend*. He was tellin' me of him the other night. Misses him a great deal, Oi think. He come in the public bar for a drink to take upstairs wid 'un, and if you don't mind Oi sayin' so, Mrs. Bolitho, he did seem in some state. He's been havin' a bit of a tussle with they Verrans who've been staying at Lanoe since old Mrs. Bryant passed on. Reckon they do scare 'un somehow. He kept mentioning this *friend* of his to Vancouver. How he did wish

he'd come over. But now he've got you, Oi do reckon he's feelin'
much better. Much less 'mazed, as it were."

It was Alyson's turn to ask questions. She was familiar with the
dialect word for confusion and very much wanted to know just how
"'mazed" the landlord of the Cornish Arms found Davey. For that
matter, just how emotionally undone he had allowed himself to
appear before such strangers.

"I hope he didn't sound too distraught. I know our aunt's burial
was very upsetting for him. And then to find strangers actually living
in her house—that came as a complete shock, you know. My cousin's
getting on, as you can see. Things affect him more than they used to.
Then I suspect that's true of all of us as we get older." She smiled
toothily at the publican. "Your turn will come, Mr. Pascoe."

The object of her remarks leaned even more over the wooden
bar flap that partitioned the small gap separating the guest room
from the public bar. He cocked his head as he devoured her words.
"Right you are, ma'am! But with Mr. Bryant Oi've had the impression it didn' stop there. With the Verrans, that is. He's also been on
about your aunt and her sister."

"Sister-in-law," Alyson corrected.

He ignored that. "Not at all happy about the two o' *them*, he was.
Then he went on about our vicar and what he did know about Mrs.
Bryant and her troubles. Nor were even that end on't. Your cousin
been see'd on the moors ever day, Oi reckon. And come back much
the worse for it. The daily who cleans here and has been doin' his
room says he be allus talkin' to himself. An' that b'aint the end of
it, neither. While Oi got this chance to talk wi'd 'ee, Oi reckon 'tis
me duty to say your cousin wasn' at all nice wi' them TV people
when they was filmin' to these parts. Accused 'em, he told me himself, of ruinin' Cornwall by encouraging more and more tourists,
which is what we do all live off, ma'am, if 'ee don' moind Oi sayin'
so. And to add to all on that, he do reckon they've been bringin'
people back from the dead, all the way from King Arthur and his

toime, jest to plague on 'ee and to do harm to the loikes on you. Now Oi ask on 'ee, ma'am, don' that sound like someone what isn' well? Truth is, Mrs. Bolitho, Oi and me missus is glad to have you come. Oi reckon then there's no wife he's got over there you might suggest come to Pentudy and, loike, help to straighten of 'un out?"

Alyson was appalled. She was also afraid of how far all this had gone. First things first, though, she told herself. "I think I told you, Mr. Pascoe, that my cousin is a bachelor. But I'll speak with his friend, the one with whom he's lived for many years. So I suggest you put your mind at rest. My cousin is in good hands, and I'll rally the family if and when such proves to be needed."

Pascoe leaned back a little. He felt quite satisfied with getting all that off his chest. Only one thing remained, however, and he toyed with the notion of spinning it in the silly cow's direction. "So your loony cousin is a fairy, too" was what he had in mind to say. But he thought better of it and asked instead whether she would like another cider.

FIFTEEN

Dearest Davey:

Your phone call bothered me and I am replying immediately. It just didn't *sound* like you. You kept pausing, and that certainly didn't sound like my Davey! You didn't even ask how Wacky Bennett is getting on since he had the lame leg. Has your Cornish "memory lane" trip made you forget all you've left behind? And I don't just mean your cat. Don't tell me it was that Methodist burial that upset you. You've been to far worse here. Remember the Italian wedding when the groom passed out his business card going down the aisle?

More seriously, I really don't like the idea of your getting caught up in some legal business where you could so easily find yourself out of your depth. Knowing you, my dear—how you *loathe* all talk about wills and your refusal to ever give a thought to litigation— my instinct was to fly right over and check things out. But as I said to you earlier this evening, your cat has been limping and I felt a visit to the vet was imperative. I might even phone the twenty-four-hour people.

I think the idea of getting Alyson to join you might be a good one. But make damn sure she doesn't come armed with those kids who so get up your ass. Also, and *write this down, Davey*, make sure she brings that paper with Hannah's deposition on it. Don't do anything with it immediately. I mean, don't show it to the Verrans or anything like that. And, for Christ's sake, *don't lose it!* I'll be in contact before you need to make any new move. It's obvious to me they're bluffing, but it takes a certain legal skill to call that bluff. Which, of course, is where I'll come in. I'll need a little time to bone up on the British law over wills and inheritances, but that's no big deal.

And now, sweetheart, keep your cool and remember I love you and think of you all the time.

"I know that, darling, so now give me that back and I'll put it in my vast collection of love letters. How often these days does someone receive a letter the same day its author joins him?" Davey held out his hand for the stationery from which Ken had been reading, up there in what was now their shared room in the Cornish Arms. "So how *is* Wacky Bennett doing? I think of him all the time. There are so many bloody cats around here, it's hard not to. But some of these are black and malevolent. There was one at the vicarage I wouldn't want to meet on a dark night. And I bet those Frocins have one and always have."

"You know cats," Ken said quickly. "The moment I arranged to take him into Sechelt his limp disappeared. The old 'toothache vanishing before you hit the dentist's chair' syndrome. I got Murray McKistry from the gas station to check him and the house each day. I also told Mrs. Hermann I'd be gone for a few days and asked if she could keep an eye on everything, as well. She's very good. And you know how she dotes on that cat." His ruse succeeded. Davey changed the subject.

"I'm amazed to see you standing there, even after you called from Heathrow. Of course, you didn't have to rent a car and drive all night down here. You must be pooped. Besides, now we've got two cars rented. What did you think? I was riding around here on a bicycle?"

"Not pooped enough to hop into bed, even with you alongside," his lover said. "But first we have to have a darn good talk about what's been happening, and then we'd better huddle with Alyson and decide on a strategy vis-à-vis your dwarf friends from Tintagel. Oh, yes, by the way, I got the oddest look from the host of your jolly old Cornish Arms. I guess someone's been blabbing about my status in the Bryant family."

"Alyson," Davey muttered.

His partner didn't comment; he was by no means certain the person he was referring to wasn't in the room with him. Ken next suggested a walk. It would clear his head, he explained, after being cooped up in the car. And it would refresh his memory, as he had only visited Pentudy once before and that aeons ago. What Ken didn't mention was his brief conversation with Davey's cousin in which she'd intimated her deep concern about Davey's quite violent reactions to such topics as the Frocins, whom he refused now to call the Verrans, the BBC King Arthur series, and what he mysteriously referred to as the "Hannah and Nora situation"—all three of which he seemed convinced were mysteriously connected by Cornish spells that had been set in motion by the steady destruction of Cornwall by tourists and the ugly, ubiquitous clutter that came in their wake.

"How about a trip to the old homestead?" Ken suggested. "That's where things started to go wrong for you, wasn't it?"

Davey seemed to acquiesce, but when they reached the house he veered to the left and took the steep path leading to the stile at the corner edge of Lanoe's upper garden. "Let's see a bit of the moor first," he insisted. "It's only right that you start with the moor. After all, it's the most important thing around here. It's where everything happens."

He didn't explain that remark but, assuming his lover was in tacit agreement, trudged up the turf and clambered over the stile. From behind, Ken observed carefully. He remembered stiles from former visits to Cornwall. He smiled wryly. The last time, though, they were able to vault them.

They joined up where the carpet of heather met the cultivated termination of the Lanoe grounds. Above their heads came a hollow croaking. Davey didn't look up, recognizing ravens. He did shout out to Ken, however: "Remember the line from Shelley? 'The obscene ravens, clamorous o'er the dead'? Lots of things have died out here, and not just bodies but hopes and strange loves. I bet you dollars to doughnuts the Frocins have a pet raven."

Ken wasn't disposed to pursue the matter, but his lawyer's mind prudently recorded it. Instead he asked Davey where he was taking him as they picked their way gingerly across the rough terrain.

"This is where they must have walked each day," Davey said, suddenly stopping and pointing across a valley toward a pile of seemingly perilously piled boulders that formed one of the numerous tarns dotting the bracken-flecked landscape. "But not at the same time. One in the morning, according to the knife grinder. The other in the afternoon. Both accompanied by that poor devil of a dog, though. Then one day, with Nora dragging a reluctant Gypo down that path, Hannah came out to meet her. To take the dog from her and go on her own walk with him? To conclude some quarrel out here in the moor's privacy? Who knows? Who will ever know?"

Ken thought hard. He decided to take a risk. Somehow the moor emboldened him. It was as if the treeless spaces and the general human silence prompted confessions that closer, more populated spaces would have discouraged. "Davey, is there something you want to tell me? Is that why we're out here?"

Davey, too, contemplated taking a risk. He had, in fact, wanted to use the moorland freedom to muster his courage and think out his words before entering Lanoe House and then broach the subject of Nora's confession, right there in the room where he'd discovered her secret.

But this moor was her place, too. Had she not said so in the course of her outpouring? Had she not described the place as free of the shackles of God and demeaning moral judgement? "You remember Nora, Uncle Joseph's sister?" Davey now asked.

"You mean Hannah's bête noire?"

"I found something in her room. Something pretty shocking, as a matter of fact."

Ken waited. He had a suspicion that this moment was what he had been waiting for—not just when they were reunited in the inn's bedroom but from the moment he had detected the steely tension in his lover's voice during that startling telephone call that had precipitated his sudden trip

Alyson might think her cousin had his sense of reality assaulted by a weird blend of the unsettling intrusion of the Verrans into his life and the home of their recently dead aunt, all coincidental with his profound shock at the obliteration of the Cornwall that had formed him and shaped so much of his earlier life. Indeed, Davey may well have told her such, but Ken thought that was just the surface stuff. That this business about Nora was the key to all the rest.

He cast his fly. "Do you want to tell me what she said?" Then, remembering Davey's propensity to garnish, he held out his hand. "Better still, do you have the letter?"

His friend ignored the latter injunction and looked instead in the direction of Rough Tor where a cloud-fingering sun cast gigantic undulations across the stone-flecked countryside. "She was a dyke." Out of the corner of his eye he saw Ken stiffen and remembered how the lawyer disliked that word. "A lesbian," he substituted swiftly. "And most of her life—at least since Hannah's arrival—she was tortured out of her existence. The letter was one long scream of frustrated love. It was really horrible, Ken. Just imagine the two of them locked together in that house, with Nora repudiated at every turn!"

Ken suppressed a smile. Just like Davey to turn this into a Brontës-like melodrama. These moody moors, he reflected, had a whole lot to blame for, not least his lover's highly wrought sensibilities. His words, however, were in an altogether different mode. "It certainly would explain Hannah's constant griping," he said.

"It explains a lot more than that! If you ask me, it lies behind whatever happened out here. I think it was more than just words between them. I think it's what caused Nora to precede her sister-in-law into the Breakers. I...I think there was *violence*. What's more, I think those Frocins got it all from Hannah. That's why they were so easily able to blackmail her, get her, too, eventually into the Breakers. That's why I also think they've got us over a barrel when it comes to the possession of Lanoe."

"And all this was in the letter?" Ken couldn't keep the incredulity entirely out of his voice, nor, for that matter, a familiar sense of ordered diction. "I think you had better let me see it. Everything hangs on it if you have nothing else to go on."

Davey finally looked Ken in the eye, his expression appealing. "That's the trouble. I don't have it. Not anymore."

He explained with great care precisely what had happened. How he had searched elsewhere afterward and come up with nothing. Then he changed the subject, as if he couldn't bear hearing Ken's levelled lawyer's response to such scanty, no, nonexistent evidence. "You see the implications, don't you? If the genetic theory is true, as they say, then I could be the result of Sapphic Aunt Nora. And if me, why not Quentin and all his campy goings-on?"

But Ken wasn't in the mood for digression and a discussion of sexual inheritance. "Well, for starters, sweetheart, I'd keep all you've told me tight under your hat. Not least with your Tintagel friends, but Alyson, too. She's had enough on her plate without being told now that while her first son's a schizophrenic her second has turned out gay. But with all that said and done, if the Verrans are halfway as litigious as you seem to think, they could not only cause trouble over the property but paddle in libel waters, too. I mean, if it's implied they got first one old lady into a rest home and then the other, all by blackmail... England's hot on that, I understand. No, with that letter of yours now just dust on these moors, none of that should be even mentioned again until we're safely back in Canada, and then only to me and Wacky Bennett! Get me, Davey, *silence!*" To give emphasis, he lifted his index finger to his lips.

For a fleeting instant Davey wanted to hit Ken. Then he looked around and remembered where he was. With a shudder he turned stiffly back and headed for the safety of the village.

Ken followed some feet behind. He knew Davey was in a turmoil of pent-up frustration and hurt that he hadn't proved more supportive. But he rejoiced nevertheless. He knew that in spite of all that he had won a victory. That whatever his thoughts and suspicions over his recent experiences, Davey would now turn first and foremost to Ken to fight and argue over such matters. After all, that was what lovers were for.

Sixteen

All three of them drove in Ken's car. At Ken's invitation Alyson sat up front while Davey readily remained alone in back. For the most part, as they'd headed initially for Tintagel, they were silent—each preoccupied with his or her own thoughts. Alyson had duly given Davey Hannah's scrawled statement that they were to be her sole beneficiaries. He now patted it in his breast pocket. Ken had told him he believed it might prove useful, either when confronting the Verrans—their first proposed port of call—or subsequently the people at the Breakers who might like the extra identification of the cousins.

They were also scheduled to visit the undertakers and collect the old lady's ashes. At first the idea had been for the men to take them back to Canada and scatter them over the Pacific Ocean near their house. But they had finally agreed with Ken that they should dispose of them over the Atlantic, close to the rugged coastline where she had spent such a large portion of her life. Davey hadn't revealed Hannah's supposed Jewish ancestry, reasoning with himself that she had chosen a Methodist life and it wasn't for him to interfere with that. Besides, she'd already received a Christian burial—however inept for his taste—and he could see no purpose in contemplating some Jewish observance, even if that were feasible.

By the time they arrived at the Breakers early that afternoon, they had already flung Hannah's remains from the gaunt cliffs of Tregardock to the accompaniment of wheeling gulls but without another human in sight. The visit to the Verrans' house—Davey's Frocins—proved abortive, although they did spot the assembled TV trucks and cameras outside the Victorian bulk of King Arthur's Castle Hotel and assumed the dwarfs were currently involved with the filming of the series. Davey, certainly, wasn't keen to seek them out, and with both Alyson and Ken eager to find a decent restaurant for lunch in that touristy town, the matter wasn't pursued with any vigour.

Alyson was most keen to investigate the Breakers, feeling as she did that she had a certain competence in evaluating kindred institutions. She was also thinking of a good opportunity to divulge the fact she'd learned before breakfast that Quentin and Hester were now anxious to join the three of them as soon as possible. It was this that caused her to cast anxious glances at her cousin every now and then. However, she had decided Ken would be the first to receive the news, if that turned out to be feasible.

Ken was highly sensible to Davey's scarcely concealed agitation as they approached the large granite mansion that was the Breakers. On several occasions Ken had asked Davey what he expected to find, considering that both his aunts who had sojourned there were now dead. But each time the lawyer had gotten no clear explanation. Apart from being told the Frocins had been responsible for both women ending up in the nursing home and that perhaps the staff would be able to shed light on that, Ken remained puzzled and far from convinced the trip would prove worthwhile.

The first person the trio encountered was a Miss Foxworthy,

who announced she was the one they'd spoken to, both from Canada and on the phone the night before, and who, as matron, was in charge of the institution perched on the cliff top. Davey mused that it wasn't that far from the lonely spot where they'd recently scattered Hannah's ashes, but his reflection was disconcertingly interrupted by her very next remarks.

"My, we're popular today! At least poor old Hannah is! You're the second group of her relatives to visit what turned out to be her last abode. They're talking to Miss Fairweather at this moment. Then they always chatted with her when the Verrans came to visit their cousin. You must be the American ones, of course."

Davey strove to keep his voice even. "Canadian," he corrected. "That's me. And if I got it correctly when I was talking to those two, they're just third cousins or something. Hannah Bryant was the widow of our—" he nodded in the direction of Alyson "—Uncle Joseph. His sister, our Aunt Nora, was in this place before her, I understand."

The matron stared at him. "The Cornish use *cousin* much more frequently than perhaps you do out there."

Davey stared back. "I was born in St. Keverne. My cousin here, in Falmouth. We could hardly be more Cornish, I think."

Ken saw this as only leading to unprofitable antagonism. After all, it was they who were there to extract information, not the other way around. He extended his hand. "Well, I'm Ken Bradley and no relation whatsoever to your late patient. I also happen to have been born in the State of California. Thank you for having us here, Miss Foxworthy. I can imagine how terribly busy you must be. May I inquire how many patients you have in your charge?"

The matron adjusted her grey-haired bun. She was mollified to the degree she thought relevant to her status and the situation. "Here at Breakers we call them guests," she announced. "Thank you for asking, Mr. Bradley. We have twenty-five at present. As a matter of fact, we're worked off our feet. Staff you know—impossible to get and impossible to train when you're lucky enough to land one. Then that's life, isn't it? I like to think we're just one great big happy family at Breakers, in spite of how such decent concepts are hideously distorted nowadays, not to say ridiculed."

Despite such sentiments, Alyson didn't feel this woman to be as warm as the Anglican nuns who ran St. Bride's, only she was prepared to withhold judgement until she had seen and learned more. "Your guests must have a beautiful view when the weather holds," she added judiciously.

Alyson was vouchsafed a look from the matron, which startled her by its manifest satisfaction. Then why would Alyson know that her comment was Lydia Foxworthy's favourite lead-in to a description of her domain. "How right you are! Breakers began as a luxury hotel, you see. Fell on hard times during the slump or depression and finally reemerged after the war when I was demobbed from the Wrens and managed to get it started as a desirable place of calm and care for those desirous of a rest from the rigours of daily life."

Davey thought she'd learned her prospectus for her Breakers by heart.

"Naturally most of our guests are elderly," she continued. "But right from the start I've insisted that not be necessarily so. Your relative Nora was a case in point. Not her late sister-in-law, of course."

Davey did a rapid calculation. He concluded that Nora was no spring chicken when she entered that grim establishment, and cleared his throat preparatory to saying so. But a glance from Ken made him look out of the plate-glass window of the matron's office and down at the pounding surf.

It was Alyson, encouraged by the response from the other woman, who stated more fully the reason for their appearance. "Until your notification of Mr. Bryant, neither of us was aware that our aunt was your…your guest. Though, of course, we knew you had taken care of our Aunt Nora prior to that." Alyson then ventured on a flight of imagination, deeming it appropriate at that point. "Aunt Hannah *always* spoke so highly of your treatment of her sister-in-law." But having said that, she immediately regretted her departure from the strict truth.

"Is that so?" the matron said. "I must say it isn't the impression we received at Breakers. I'd have said there was no love lost between them, though perhaps the circumstances of Nora's death might have changed that slightly."

Three visitors mirrored glances. None of them were of the impression there had been anything unusual concerning Nora's departure.

Ken finally spoke up. "I'm afraid at my age I have a grotesquely short memory. But what was it, Matron, that could have changed, well, shall we call it Hannah's *sibling rivalry*, about her companion at Lanoe House?"

The others hung on Miss Foxworthy's response. For the smallest moment she seemed to Davey to be disconcerted. At least her grey eyes flickered. However, there was nothing in the cool, assured voice to betray her.

"Oh, I thought everyone was notified. Or rather that Hannah would have done so. Nora Bryant, you see, had a slight accident down there on the rocks. She slipped and the waves caught her. Staff got her out, but she was in a hysterical state. Her friends here at Breakers managed to calm her and get her off to bed and some much-needed sedation. She never resumed an active role in the family after that. She remained in bed, and that was where her sister-in-law saw her for the last few times left to her. There had been an unfortunate incident several years earlier when a male guest slipped and fell on the other side of our charming little cove. He drowned." She smiled deprecatingly. "In hindsight I should have acted then, but I didn't. After what befell poor Nora, though, I closed the open beach to the guests. You'll see the consequences when we embark on our little tour."

The matron's sitting room, as she called it, went strangely quiet as her somewhat stark information was duly digested. It was Ken again who broke the silence. "Matron, you mentioned Nora's friends. I was wondering…are any of them still with you? Come to that, are there any special pals of Hannah with whom we could chat?"

"That is fully my intention, Mr. Bradley. There's one in particular who befriended both women. If she's not too tired, I'll take you to her room. At the moment she's entertaining the Verrans who, as I said earlier, always stop by for a chat with her. Or did rather. I doubt whether we shall be seeing much more of them, what with your aunt's passing and their involvement with all this filmmaking of the Arthurian legends and whatnot for the BBC."

Davey was despondent. Knowing the diminutive couple, he was sure they'd wear *anyone* out, especially a patient in that place. "Is she quite old?" he asked suddenly.

"I was coming to that," he was informed crisply. "Indeed, Jenny Fairweather is *very* old. She's approaching her centenary and is quite deaf." She eyed them in her most matronly fashion. "You'll all have to speak up. And I'll tell you now, I won't allow you to fatigue her." With that schoolmistressy tone she rose. "And now if you're ready? I can hear the Verrans departing."

That horrified Davey. "But we were looking for them. It's important we see them. Especially Mr. Bradley and my cousin, Mrs. Bolitho. They've never met them. We missed them in Tintagel and I can't stress how important—"

"Well, it's quite impossible now, Mr. Bryant. If you see them, it must be out in the grounds, and that means you'll have to abandon your tour of Breakers. A highly successful institution such as this runs on well-oiled routines and careful schedules. I'm afraid I can make no exceptions." Her smile was presumably intended to sweeten her medicine, but it was patently of a saccharine substance.

Davey looked so upset that Alyson longed to cross and hold her cousin's hand, but Ken forestalled any such thing. "We'll have to see the Verrans tomorrow then. It's important that we see your Jenny, Matron. She is, after all, the closest link left to Alyson's and Davey's relatives. It can make this whole venture worthwhile."

He didn't elaborate on what that venture was for the simple reason he hadn't, as yet, decided what it might be, other than to calm Davey and alleviate his fears. And he wasn't about to ask Miss Foxworthy for a contribution to that project!

Without even looking back the matron sailed, galleon-fashion in her starched white uniform, out of her snug office and down the window-bordered corridor. The visitors obediently followed.

SEVENTEEN

J ennifer Fairweather wasn't sitting in her room but in the corridor itself—a tiny pink figure topped with snow-white hair, everybody's "grandma," at least from a distance. Closer up a different image emerged. The eyes of the retired schoolteacher were a striking blue, but frosty for much of the time. This was because, at ninety-nine, she was often irritable, even if she took certain steps to conceal it.

One abiding frustration was the world's insistence on treating her as a little old lady with premanufactured characteristics: a happy mien, a gentle temperament, and a general disposition to treat fools kindly. Another was the propensity of those in their late sixties to identify with her, whereas almost another lifetime lay infuriatingly between theirs and hers. She was also quickly put out of sorts by those—the majority—who in meeting her at once took on a cloying attitude of false sympathy and phony merriment as if they were donating her some special gift from their paltry treasury. These were the kind of people who used *we* instead of *you* when inquiring about her, in the manner often ascribed to the medical profession when dealing with elderly—and not so elderly—patients.

And if these irritants failed to rile her, then she was so often left with that desolating sense of loneliness from having bid farewell to her cherished intellectual peers with whom she could discuss such things as books, bitchy gossip, and politics. Now that she was nearly a hundred, she had also lost the vast majority of those with whom she had once shared birthdays.

The real Jennifer, currently masquerading at the Breakers as "Sweet Jenny," had been a wicked-tongued, exigent if brilliant, teacher of biology and mathematics at the highly regarded Exeter Academy for Girls who, after an excessive and sustained bout with the bottle on retiring from her beloved profession, was persuaded, if not bullied, by her devious relations to enter the Breakers and thus be conveniently shut out of the mind and conscience of those over whom she had never taken pains to disguise her contempt or disdain.

The real Jennifer also harboured a lively animosity toward the illiterate staff who now nursed her wasted body and starved mind. She would have liked to extend this antipathy toward that fatuous entity of starchy pomposity and maudlin sentiment who called herself Matron, but over the years Jenny had seen the whip of authority coil and slash, the steely voice grow even harder with malice when sloppy clichés no longer served their purpose. Somewhere along the way an atavistic fear overtook her irritation thereby causing a novel caution to inform her words and prudent conduct to be manifest whenever Lydia Foxworthy loomed menacingly on her horizon. Jenny often told herself she was a survivor; otherwise, as she also told herself, she wouldn't have lasted as long as she had. The old lady was quite convinced that her lofty geriatric status had as much to do with her mental state as with the luck of her physical well-being.

As the group now approached, Jenny's spirits sank. This lot weren't about to prove as enjoyable as her friends, the dwarfs, who always stimulated her by their honed malice and profound suspicion of anyone taller than they, with the exception of such wizened and ancient flesh as she represented.

Two of them, she noted, were men with white hair, while the head of the rotund woman accompanying them was solidly grey. As for the corseted figure in uniform, she had no fear today of her, knowing that Matron wouldn't linger. After excessive introductions and patronizing her oldest source of income in the place, she would amble off to some less boring situation such as bullying her nurses or counting her coffers.

It all went very much like that, though Jenny couldn't know, of course, whether her enemy eventually found a subordinate as victim, some hapless inmate, or drew solace from her wall safe or ledgers.

"So you're Hannah's young relatives. Knew her for years, I did. That is, I mean before she joined our—" she drew breath and revealed toothless gums "—happy family of guests at bloody Breakers."

They all laughed dutifully, remembering the matron's earlier admonition about what the inhabitants of Breakers were called. Jenny decided to sound them out further. She had long ago learned the lesson of disloyalty to her chief custodian or, equally, the danger of making ribald remarks about the institution itself. Visitors like this lot could talk, had too often turned out to be sneaky tale bearers to those in charge.

"I was only saying to my friends, the Verrans, earlier this afternoon—"

"Our cousins," Alyson volunteered, incurring a hostile look from Davey and an encouraging one from Ken.

Not that such expressions registered. Another lesson from a long life that Jenny had learned was that you pressed on regardless, otherwise people verbally ran over you. "Was that how lucky we all are to have found this place, especially if everything had gone wrong outside, everything soured."

"You do have a beautiful view," Ken said, fearing she might go off on some boring tangent as he'd experienced with other geriatric cases.

The blue eyes duly frosted, like a conditioned reflex. That was the kind of idiotic observation she expected from those who, on noticing the turned-down corners of her mouth due to the long absence of dentures, thought she was in perpetual need of cheering up.

"The staff do their best to relieve the boredom, and some of the younger ones tell me the food is more or less palatable. I wouldn't know as my taste buds have long departed. But over the years I've made friends and have had them die on me. Hannah Bryant, whom I believe you say is your relative, was one such."

"Davey has just attended her funeral as her only nephew," Ken supplied. "Could you tell us a little about her life here? She often came and stayed with us in Canada before her incarceration here."

Jenny enjoyed his emphasis and decided to forgive his stupid observation about the view. "I knew her before she became another shut-in, you see. At first it was as a visitor when she came to see her sister-in-law."

The old woman licked her lips, partly in pleasurable anticipation of unfolding that drama of misunderstanding, partly because she was given to drooling. She was encouraged by the fact that they had seated themselves in a horseshoe, their three heads craned forward to drink up her revelations.

The matriarch of the Breakers smoothed her pink nightie, confident she now had their attention, and prepared to deliver what was more or less a repetition of what she'd earlier told the Verrans. It was a saga she had skillfully shaped over many hours staring out at that unfathomable sea while her aching body bid her turn her mind inward, and which had gratifyingly gripped the Verrans' razor-sharp imaginations as their little bodies had sat stiffly before her.

For one fleeting but precious moment then she had returned to thoughts of school and her pupils in that long-ago classroom. But Len had belched, Hilda had snorted her disapproval, and the nostalgia was immediately banished.

Unfortunately, glancing at perspiring Alyson and her seemingly invert menfolk, no comparable image was forthcoming. She decided to crispen the details and furnish a little psychological reflection that, in her experience, men like these tended to relish.

"I shouldn't say I understood Hannah right away. To the contrary, I couldn't make head nor tail of her at first. She was so different from me, and I don't mean in our ages. But she turned out to be closer to me than most of them here. She could at least remember the General Strike and what the dole was. Or pretended to. I could never be sure when she was merely trying to identify with me, as she took to me right off the bat and wanted to please me, which is more than I can say she wanted to do for her sister-in-law."

"They didn't always get on," Alyson contributed rather superfluously.

The look her comment received was pure "schoolmarm." However, it wasn't accompanied by a verbal rebuke, as Jenny was saving such for a time when her audience might possibly grow more restless.

"I don't know how you perceived Hannah Bryant, of course, but from the very first I saw the romantic in her." She paused fractionally for that to sink in. It had signally failed to do so with the dwarfs, and she suspected with their relatives it would be likewise. She was far from sure that any of them knew what a romantic really was. Jenny had rashly invoked the term *Dionysian* to several people in the Breakers in connection with the matron's concealed appetites, and her observation had received a stony blank in response, save in the case of the hoydenish young nurse who thought she was mispronouncing the word *diarrhea*.

Ken nodded encouragingly at her, Davey frowned with disbelief, and Alyson looked so blank that the old lady was quite unable to read her. In fact, the only mother among them had just stolen a moment to reflect that perhaps both Quentin and Hester would have liked to hear the precise English and well-modulated allocution of this ancient person. She also took time to wish that her offspring were a little better-spoken and not given to the adulterated Cockney that seemed to have affected the upper classes of their whole generation.

"Hannah was what you might call the quintessential romantic," Jenny continued. "No wonder she loved those moors when she saw a gnome or piskie peeking out from behind every boulder!" The old woman was beginning to enjoy herself. None of them had as yet objected to any word she'd used, and *quintessential* was up there with *Dionysian* and *romantic* itself as among her current favourites.

"You might call it the attraction of opposites. My background is scientific, you see. I am the trained scientist who on hearing the word *moor* thinks at once of mineral ores like tin and copper and their alloy bronze. And historically at once springs to mind the Mesolithic, Neolithic, and Megalithic peoples."

Ken clapped and was once more relegated to the status of oaf by the speaker.

"Nor could I ever understand her attitude toward her dog, Gypo, who she adored and I think offered greater affection than she did to her own kind. Mind you, I have to say the same of Nora with whom she shared the animal." Jenny drew needed breath.

"I think the dog was Nora's and that Hannah was allowed to exercise it," Davey interjected. "Hannah gave it to her as a present and then sort of reneged on the business." He sighed with relief from at least getting that amount of information bequeathed by his aunt's note off his chest.

Jenny scowled at him. "Be that as it may. We shan't quibble with the small amount of time we have available. A pity, however, that you were not here to see the result of the dog's violent biting of both of them. That was what brought Nora here in the first place. Her limbs were savaged and her face mutilated. She lost the use of her left eye, and her upper lip never healed satisfactorily right up to the time she attempted to take her life out there."

She leaned back, Davey's intrusion dealt with and attention

restored. "If Hannah was the poet, and I have much of her verse here in my room should you be interested, Nora was the stoic, down-to-earth Cornishwoman who understood her calling and I'm afraid rather resented Hannah's attentions toward her. The poetic fancy, if you will, that animated so much of her response to her late husband's sister as well as all those villagers whom she regarded as dour and materialistic, so close in their grubby imaginations to the beasts they tended."

"We would indeed love to see Hannah's verses!" Ken exclaimed. "And anything else she might have written, come to that."

Davey was so surprised at the old woman's revelations that he had to shake his head to get his own words out. "But that's all the wrong way round!" he practically shouted. "It was Nora who was so wounded by Hannah's failure to respond to her."

Alyson didn't like any of this. She thought she saw hitherto unseen veins begin to mould on Jenny's tight-skinned forehead, a scraggy neck begin to wobble perilously. "Oh, please go on, Miss Jenny. We are all so indebted to the trouble you're taking." Her voice was almost a wail, and it was that which quelled her two companions.

"Nora was my soul mate from the time of her arrival. She poured out her frustration at being unable to respond to Hannah's so-passionate nature. She found her own solace in the moor, not as a place of magic but as somewhere to escape her sister-in-law's endless pleas and desire that they be closer. I knew her much longer, of course, than Hannah. For more sustained periods of time we were able to talk and comment on life. But when Hannah came in permanently and we were able to sit here we knew almost right away that we were going to hit it off. It wasn't long after that I learned from her how poor Nora went off her head out there near Rough Tor and accused Hannah of being cruel to their mutually loved Gypo.

"As so often in life, neither of them were wholly to blame for the dog's nervous breakdown, for that is what appears to have happened to their Irish setter. If you want my opinion, and I presume that's why you sought me out, they both in their different ways blamed the moor for their enmity. Nora claimed Hannah insulted it by what she called her sister-in-law's banal poesy involving legends and lore. Hannah, on the other hand, insisted Nora could only count minerals and dates and never see the beauty of the total picture. But what they both did was to use it for their own purposes as a weapon in their mutual warfare.

"It's the strangest thing—that great big blank of cultivation that has been hymned and worshipped by mankind since the earliest times, used by two unknown women in the twentieth century for the most pedestrian of purposes. You couldn't dissuade either of them from their attitudes, not only of the moor but of everything else. They were just poles apart. I should know, shouldn't I? I had the confidence of both of them when they ended up here."

She had barely stopped, running out of breath and energy rather than words, when her visitors started up.

"We didn't know we were going to meet you, Jenny," Ken asseverated warmly. "But believe me it's a privilege, and to see those papers Hannah left you will be an extra one."

Jenny got up, wobbled, and then with her hand to the wall tottered the few feet to her bed.

Alyson addressed her widow's hump that so cruelly arched her back. "I feel very close to Aunt Hannah. From just a little girl and paying annual visits I loved the moorland landscape. Davey knows that. I hope my children can learn to love them, too."

Only Davey was silent. He didn't even enter the little room as Jenny gave Ken the promised package from under her mattress. From the linoleum carpeted corridor, over the persistent sound of the surf, he heard the old lady insist they keep the stuff, declaring that at her age she was no longer minded to retain possessions.

EIGHTEEN

For the journey back to Pentudy and the Cornish Arms, Ken and Alyson voted that Davey drive. They insisted only he knew the shortcuts through the rustic, most unspoiled lanes, and he consented when he realized he would be allowed to concentrate on his driving and not be involved with their conversation.

It was this he wanted most. Shaken by the old woman's interpretation of his aunts' relationship, he was also developing another, equally startling theory. He was now of the opinion that she was in cahoots with his Frocins, had probably been paid by them to tell a wholly fictitious story about Hannah and even provided her papers to hand over to them and further confuse matters.

But for the most part, Davey was sunk in deep melancholy. He still believed in Nora's outpouring of grief but nursed the bleak conviction that after the old girl's intervention it was more and more unlikely he would ever convince his lover, let alone the woman sitting beside him, as they duly entered a lane bordered not by billboards but by wind-scorched gorse and grotesquely bent sloe bushes.

However, when Alyson could contain herself no longer and suddenly proclaimed the imminent arrival of her children, he made no protest. Abruptly, in the manner notions so often visited him, and even while she was nervously announcing Quentin's name, he saw his honorary "nephew" as possibly his last chance to corroborate his now-solid conviction that his gay genes and those of the teenager had descended from the unhappy woman who had died without ever knowing sexual fulfillment from her heart's desire.

Alyson, though registering fleeting relief that her cousin wasn't going to prove "difficult," was occupied with something quite other. "Do you know what I think?"

Her question went unanswered. Davey was too busy making plans as to how he would skillfully cross-examine Quentin in the manner he had seen his lawyer lover use; Ken was consumed with going through the sheaf of notebook leaves Jenny had handed him.

"I think there was something fishy about that place," Alyson forged on. "I didn't trust that woman from when we first set eyes on her. She had such cold eyes! And her smile was so phony. And did you notice the corridor was always empty? Not another inmate in sight, or nursing staff, either. I think that matron hardly has any staff. For that matter I can't see anyone wanting to work under her. I imagine she can be very bossy when it suits her purpose. I also got the impression the old lady thought so, too. Nor does everything stop there. What if there's not only a lack of nurses but to deal with that she has all her patients under sedation? When the poor dears are lying asleep in their beds all the time, they're so much easier to deal with. I...I learned about that at St. Bride's."

To get her from that painful topic rather than from any conviction over her theory, Davey spoke up. "Old Jenny sure didn't seem drugged. For someone of her age she was remarkably *with* it. She certainly hadn't lost her marbles, though I wouldn't be surprised if she's in the pay of the Frocins. Those people would stop at nothing!"

Ken stopped rustling Hannah's papers on his lap. "Here's one of the poems Jenny mentioned. I guess you'd call it romantic, though it has its dollop of self-pity." He read her words in a declamatory voice.

"The Moor's mercuric enemy,
That lethal, leaden mist
Doth suffocate my mind tonight.
My head again afire with fear, seeped
From the overwhelming might
Of well-honed Cornish hate;
Malingering still beyond these leaded panes,
Down from the dusk when fear stirred
In dark air laced with bats and owls
And called my wedding night!
My woman's slit unloved
Became a festering wound.
Unfed, these griefs have raised a septic barrier;
Now sour silence cuts me off,
And wordless spite imprisons me with her.
I am made captive within these granite walls
(And even colder slate).
Denied me yet again:
The nippled ridge, the silvered cleansing stream
Of Rough Tor's healing moon."

When he finished, Ken seemed rather embarrassed, so much so that Davey turned his head and looked at him anxiously. But his partner was already scrambling the papers again. "Boy, she sure didn't like Nora, did she? Listen to this, though it's just as much a defence of that poor bastard of a dog they fought over. No poetry here!

"Why, oh, why did she take it out on poor Gypo instead of me? I was the one she hated, not that poor darling creature. I would feed him, and she would feed him again. Always double portions of food, which he gobbled up just to please us both. Endlessly brushed and groomed till his skin was chafed and sour from four vigorous hands. The bewilderment of opposing commands—can you imagine it! Then at night, every night, summer and winter, year after tormented year, he'd be called from bed to bed at the far reaches of that large house. A human, maybe a man, would have settled for a third quarter, a place of his own. But Gypo's great love didn't permit of that kind of compromise. He padded from one to the other through the dark, and only howled if a door was slammed out of spite to prevent his return.

Why then did he single me out to bite in the end the way he did? I am happy to report that he savaged the cheek of that possessive bitch and that she never saw again with her left eye. But I am still left with the horror of their emptying that shotgun into him, leaving him to writhe and die at the back door of Lanoe at the end of a rope. They thought the dark stain soaking in his fur was my blood, but I know it was hers. That it was already there out on the moor when Gypo stood in triumph over her torn skirt and flesh, gobs of froth on his black lips, howling his hatred of her like a banshee.

But they murdered him because they believed her lies that he wanted me dead. It was her, though, he wanted destroyed when his great heart broke. She who tortured him to the point he ended up not knowing what he was doing. May the Great God of All Creatures forgive her, now that she is gone and will never plague him nor me again."

Even Ken realized that was inappropriate for reading out loud in the car. The silence was unbearable. "I'm…I'm sorry," he muttered. "That wasn't fair to her. It obviously wasn't meant for anyone to hear."

Alyson heaved her weight with a gigantic sigh. "How dreadful! How terribly sad the two of them were. Of course, none of us ever realized…"

NINETEEN

I t was Ken who had to remind sleepy cousins the next morning that they were scheduled to try again to see the Verrans and take care of that situation once and for all. Responsive to the general upbeat in spirits, even Davey now seemed more at ease. Alyson, again emboldened, suggested that, since the children would be arriving that evening in Tintagel by bus, perhaps they could kill two birds with one stone. She was unopposed.

The trip was infinitely more merry than the return the day previous. Davey and Alyson started to sing a song they had shared in childhood and which was inspired by the early emergence of the sun as they reached the coast road and their first glimpse of the sea. "The sun has got its hat on and it's coming out today, the sun has got its hat on so we shout hip-pip hooray!"

They all laughed aloud at the words and then took turns pointing at what attracted their interest while studiously avoiding the commercial constituents that didn't. The blithe mood was sustained as they rolled down the slope of Tintagel's main street past the fourteenth-century manor house with its wildly undulating roof, now called "the old post office."

Nor were they set back by discovering the Verrans finally at home in their lair. Indeed, Len, who came to the front door set in its glass porch, brought an involuntary smile to Davey who had hitherto tended to respond to the little man with a scowl. This time, though, Davey thought how much Len had come to resemble Mr. Toad in *The Wind in the Willows*. For one thing he was wearing a bright yellow waistcoat under a vivid green ascot, which Davey thought highly appropriate for the Kenneth Grahame character. But it wasn't only a sartorial transformation the little man had experienced. Gone was the antagonism, the scarcely veiled rudeness.

Instead Len beamed at the three of them, invited them into the glassed-in porch where there were cushioned wicker chairs for them to sit (he was still Cornish, after all, Davey thought, remembering), took Alyson's plump hand in both of his, and continually pumped that of Ken as if he were flushing the heads aboard ship.

All the time he talked. "Well, am Oi glad you been and found your ole cousins then. B'aint nothing loike family when it do come to sharin' good news."

He nodded affably in Davey's direction. "You do know, of course, Cousin Davey, that Hilda and Oi have become what 'ee might call the stars of this here BBC feature series that have already got world roights and a whole lot more, Oi'm told. We'm now the Frocins round here. Fact is, Hilda and me is considering gettin' the name changed, official loike. What they do call the deed poll? Then perhaps you b'aint heard of 'un over there. But you, Missus Alyson, you would know what Oi do mean. Oi tell 'ee, 'tis real nice to get some respect from some of these people. People what is now all ears and offerin' to do this and that what was snickerin' like behind our backs." He laughed, and by the way his eyes watered, Davey wondered whether he'd been drinking, separating himself perhaps from his Methodist background.

"Oh, no, my friends, tidn' the same no more. Tidn' the same at all! You should see um stare when Oi give 'em part of me speech. Started with jest a line here and there. But now we got hundreds a lines. Hilda, too, for that matter. But she do have trouble rememberin' of they. That's what her's doin' up in her room roight now. Oi'll a fetch of her in a jiffy. Got to remember the other's loines, too, you see. That's how you do know as to when to come in. Mr. Gawthrop do shout 'Camera!' and away we do go."

The little man hopped back to the opposite side of the porch and held his lapels. "Gotta imagine Oi in them medie-heaval clothes, you! One lot's bright yellow, brighter than this here waistcoat. Another is in flaming red. Hilda do say Oi'm a proper eye-catcher in that! But she's tell on 'ee when her do come down from rememberin' her loines."

He struck a ludicrous pose they could only suppose would be dealt with by the film director later. "T'other actor do say, 'Is this humpbacked dwarf the work of your auguries? May he never see the face of God, who having found you, does not drive his spear into your body!'" Len winced melodramatically, as if physically assaulted. "At the hour of Prime King Mark has a ban cried through his land t'gather up the men of Cornwall. And they all come at me with a great noise, all of them weepin' except me, the Dwarf of Tintagel."

Ken began the clapping and dutifully the others joined in. Len beamed. But the noise must have disturbed his spouse for she quickly appeared. It was immediately evident that the turn of success that had transformed her husband had had less influence on her.

"So it's you lot," she said, acknowledging Davey and nodding brusquely at his companions. "You'm the London one," she said to Alyson. Then, directing her words to Ken, she asked, "And you would be the one from over there?"

Whatever else she intended to say was frustrated by her husband, whose geniality slipped somewhat for a moment. "They'm here to congratulate us, Hilda. They come all the way here to do that."

At least that deflected her. "Staying to Lanoe House then?"

"They won't be doing that until the will is probated, will you?" Ken inquired of his companions. "We have the documents Alyson brought down with her. We'll be staying at the Cornish Arms until I can leave things in the hands of a fellow lawyer. Just a day or so as it's all straightforward. Shouldn't take long."

"Well," Hilda said, "we was glad to help the old lady as well we could. And look after the house that was frankly fallin' to pieces as neither of they was what you'd call housekeepers."

Len flicked imaginary dust off his vest. "Moind what that Jack Pascoe do charge on 'ee. He got quite a reputation, that innkeeper have. That's why we stayed on at Hannah's place whenever we was over. Course, we was watchin' our pennies then. Frankly the ole gal couldn't have started failin' at a worse time, what with the price of property being what it was and that."

Hilda resumed her familiar role; at least it was familiar to Davey right from their first conversation after the funeral service. "Oh, come on, our Len. They don' want to hear all our troubles and all we did for Cousin Hannah. They'm busy people what with all this will-making and that."

But nothing was about to abash her mate anymore. "Well, luvvy, that were all Verran matter, Oi do moind. Tidn' for ole Frocin, Oi'm tellin' 'ee." He then ignored her and addressed the visitors. "Tidn' official, but Oi heard today this Arthur business have turned out so well the Corporation have got other ideas for us. Then Oi been talkin' to the British Midgets Association. You'd be surprised what linkups is there. We little people is worldwide, you, and them what got the talent like us can maike a pretty penny!"

Hilda wasn't altogether vanquished. She snorted.

"It b'aint all sunk in for the wife," Len explained. "But it will, it will!"

Alyson looked at her watch, already anxious about the bus,

though there were still hours before it was due. Davey took the clue and stood. Ken did likewise, but this time he refrained from extending his hand to be pumped in farewell.

Outside, knowing they were still being observed, they walked sedately toward the car. Inside, however, as they drove off, they chortled and Davey shrieked. It was as if a great weight had been taken off his shoulders. In a way it had, but the problem of Frocin had some time been surpassed by his new sense of affinity with his Aunt Nora and his feeling of powerlessness to convince anyone else of the truth of her nature and therefore of her true relation to Aunt Hannah.

At a loss for what to do to fill in the space before the bus's advent, they decided to visit King Arthur's Castle where the Verrans' triumphs were in the process of being carried out. At least that was Davey's ardent wish and the others indulged him.

Around the Iron Age forts and ruins of the thirteenth-century battlements a gale howled competitively with the roar of the Atlantic many feet below as the three staggered over slippery, windshorn turf. Finally, as renewed forces of driving rain turned grey slate black, they began to think of shelter. Alyson found a cleft in the crumbling wall, but it would only hold one. The two men nodded to her, acknowledging her permission before clambering up the hill toward a rickety footbridge and several gaps in the hillside that might have been part of the ancient barrow placarded by Ministry of Works notices and those of the National Trust.

Alyson wasn't worried about their finding a comparable spot to where she huddled dry, and enjoyed the rest from the exertion of climbing. Crouched there, she vaguely remembered walking among those cliff-top ruins as a child and even recalled her anxiety then as the two families had wandered higher and higher, as her cousin was doing now, onto a terrain where the open ocean came into view but where precipitous cliffs with their face a mass of jagged slate swept down to the locked waters frothed in violent anger and strange noises came up from partially concealed caves that served as perpetual wind tunnels. She had grown progressively frightened and slipped her hand into the warm comfort of that of her older cousin.

Davey was vaguely remembering the same experience, though goaded more by the necessity of finding shelter for himself and his lover. But Ken's mind was set on wholly other matters. He was glad of the temporary separation from Alyson, for he was most anxious to have Davey to himself. This was not merely to assure him that though he might not have their immediate support over his belief the Verrans were his nemesis and whether his aunt was or wasn't a lesbian, both Ken and Alyson, each in their own fashion, were devoted to him.

They soon found a spot that Davey could see was out of the rain and Ken concluded was hidden from the public footpath. In there it was quite dark, and in the sheer proximity of their persons Ken's thoughts changed. He had just been about to whisper encouragingly to his companion of over forty years how much he still admired and respected him, indeed, how glad he was that he'd surrendered to impulse.

As Ken started to move toward Davey, he suddenly felt his lover's pressure in response as Davey instinctively sought the retired lawyer's warmth and protection with outstretched arms. It wasn't admiration or respect that welled in Ken; it was the sweet-bitter sensation of love.

Four lips met, and rain-moist garments pressed hard against each other; a stranger peering into the mouth of the shallow cave would have observed two elderly gents kissing and possibly been shocked by the incongruity of that image. But it was of no concern to either Davey or Ken. They had found the comfort of communication that began where words left off.

Davey surrendered the endlessly fomenting stew of his disillusion, paranoia and unfocused apprehension upon hearing his Ken tell him how much he loved him over and over. Ken, for his part, felt the guilt of bossiness melt away.

With the perpetual capriciousness of the Cornish climate, the sun suddenly streamed through the crevices of clouds, the turf steamed, and the wind relented. They had barely unlocked and returned to the rehabilitated October afternoon when Alyson appeared red-faced from exertion but with a smile lighting her face as she saw the two of them. "Oh, good!" she said. "I think if we start back to the car now we shall be in perfect time to meet them."

In return, lit by the glow of their fleeting experience, the two men beamed at her and exuberantly agreed it was time to meet the younger generation. As if circumstance were anxious to join the newly benign weather, the Royal Blue bus drew up almost coincidentally with their own arrival. Quentin and Hester were the first of the scattering of passengers to alight, but before they had a chance to cast around for the trio Alyson had promised them would be there, their mother stumbled out of the car and rushed to embrace them.

Ken smiled at Davey. "It's another kind of love from ours, of course, but she's sure got it in spades for them, hasn't she?"

TWENTY

I t wasn't only the weather that continued the next day to be fortuitous. Davey was dying to implement his plan and scrutinize for gay clues the young man who had now joined their party, but it was really arranged for him by the others.

It didn't happen at once, though. The Fates, as Davey Cornishly knew, weren't that facilely obedient to human interests. Or, as his mother had never been tired of telling him, unknowingly using the words of the medieval German monk, Thomas à Kempis, "Man proposes but God disposes."

At the request of the children the party was to attend the beach at Polzeath in the afternoon where they could enjoy surf-bathing and perhaps snorkelling off Pentire Head. Quentin and Hester had been careful to bring the requisite equipment with them.

Before that, though, Alyson proposed a visit to Lanoe House. Now reassured there would be no opposition from the Verrans—who had seemed strangely uninterested since good fortune had visited them from another direction—she was anxious to see the house that would eventually fall to her son and daughter. Ken was likewise eager, but in his case he told himself his primary motive was largely morbid; he was quite keen to revisit the place in which he had once nearly frozen to death (as Hannah had brought them indifferent coffee and a biscuit tin revealing mouse droppings), but which now loomed in interest as the literally bloody battleground where the two female gladiators had locked in combat and in doing so caused the death of the one creature both had apparently loved—the dog Gypo.

Of the seniors in the group, only Davey had expressed reluctance to make a return to the place that had been so unsettling for him recently. He again opted for the moors and the enjoyment of what good weather might remain during their stay. To his surprise it was Quentin who volunteered to accompany him. Sister Hester, reluctant to compete with her brother as always, elected to accompany her mother and Ken whom she didn't know well and who fascinated her by what she already detected as his probing mind masked by an old-fashioned courtliness that was entirely foreign to her.

Davey and Quentin hadn't reached the top of the Lanoe gardens—after a noisy farewell that must have been heard all over Pentudy—before the Canadian had decided where to take his young relation amid the folds and mounts of the moor. When they arrived at the point he and Ken had reached after they experienced their painful conversation about the true nature of Nora, Davey decided to pursue the specific plan that had been gradually formulating in his head as they trudged over the heather.

Rough Tor with its distinct crater stood away to their right, but it wasn't its craggy slopes to which Davey wished to steer his companion who now proved agreeably full of questions his auditor was well able to answer. Indeed, right from the outset and the crowding of them all into the car in Tintagel, when he must have surely been weary from the long coach ride from London, the boy had been remarkably affable and devoid of the uppity manner that had been so characteristic of him when Davey visited on that afternoon in Notting Hill, which now seemed centuries ago.

"There's something you might like to see about a half mile farther on," Davey said. "It's beyond that smoke you can see to your right."

"Is the moor on fire? Is that usual?" The boy seemed a mite anxious.

Davey reassured him. "They've been burning back the gorse. It's called swayling. If they didn't do that each autumn, it would be everywhere."

That seemed to reassure the youngster. At any rate he changed the subject. "I wish I'd brought Nigel. He'd have loved a run out here. At least I think he would, though I believe he's afraid of heights and this ground might prove rough for his feet."

"The poor Irish setter of your two great-aunts was out here a lot. In fact, too much. He ended up with bleeding paws." Davey was about to add that Gypo also went mad and attacked the women, but thought better of it. "I used to spend a lot of my time out here when I was your age and younger. Actually, where I'm taking you is where a funny thing happened to me."

Quentin eyed him a trifle oddly. "Nothing dangerous, I hope. I'm a total coward, you know." There was a twinkle to his eyes, which Davey noticed for the first time were almost as blue as those of old Jenny in the Breakers. However, Quentin's didn't look as if they were about to frost over.

Davey took in the blond locks tossing in the faint breeze. "I hope it isn't too bracing for you up here. I keep forgetting that people can find it cold. It's an odd thing. Back home I often shiver and complain to Ken about the temperature. But the minute I'm back on the moor, that all goes. It's as if I've never moved away. I think it's the only part of Cornwall I can say that about anymore!"

The boy glanced in the direction Davey had indicated. "What kind of thing was it that happened to you and where did it take place exactly?"

"See the stone funnel that looks like a tower? The one broken at the top and with the bracken growing right up to it? That's where it happened, and it had to do with sheep, though I didn't know that at first. Lanolin—do you know what that is?"

Quentin did. It had come up only that week in school. "Substance found on sheep's wool. Extracted and used as a base for ointments and cosmetics. I don't think I'd wear it, though. Too aggressive for me."

The comment registered with Davey. However, he continued. "It was pitch-dark, or I thought so when I first climbed inside. And I thought I recognized the smell but wasn't sure. The only thing I knew was that it had to do with animals of some kind."

They reached the base of the tall tower; it turned out to be stinging nettles at the foot not the bracken Davey had supposed. The two walked round to the west side where there was a rough wooden door in two parts, an upper and lower. The latter hung open and was broken. Davey noticed it was held together at one point with several strands of binder cord.

Apart from his earlier remarks, Quentin now seemed keen to explore. He clambered onto a boulder and peered inside. "It isn't totally dark," he called back. "Just dim. Can we go in?"

"Mind the shaft toward one edge," Davey warned. "That's why this gate's here. Too many sheep and moorland ponies have fallen in and broken a leg or something."

But before he could get all that out his young companion had disappeared inside. Davey immediately followed. It was darker in there than Quentin had suggested—at least to Davey's older eyes. He said as much. "It's darker in here than I thought. For God's sake look out for that shaft. We both must!"

"Here," Quentin said, reaching out a hand, "this will bring you to the edge. There's still a faint pong of lanolin now, but no sheep. Only little us!"

Davey swore then as he swore to himself afterward that he

strove to bring back the sheep scent from his childhood past, fought to keep everything at that level before gently drawing his young relative out about his most intimate predilections. But it wouldn't stay that way, not his feelings, that is. At least for very long.

What he now smelled was the boy-fresh body of the teenager standing next to him, just as he felt the hot hand and imagined somewhere below them, the hairy nude legs sprouting from Quentin's khaki shorts that the boy had worn for the first time that morning.

"I bet all sorts of things could happen in here. You're quite cut off from the world, aren't you?" Quentin's voice seemed to have changed.

Davey thought it was more husky. He began to babble. "This was a silver mine. Cornwall produced a lot of silver until the bottom fell through the market. Places like Malaya took over. South America, too."

"I want to grab a look down the shaft. Hold on tight to me, won't you? Hold me by the waist, Davey, and I can bend over."

Quentin had occasionally used only his first name bereft of family title, but at that moment his second cousin couldn't remember such. He dutifully clasped the young man as indicated but felt undutiful sweat break out sticky on his forehead. At the same time his knees began to tremble. He knew what that was. However long ago the last experience, he knew the onslaught of lust.

"I can just see something shining," the boy said. "Would that be water? It couldn't possibly be silver ore, could it?"

But by now Davey was impervious to questions and comments, including those he had proposed to ask himself. In a mindless fashion he was praying. He was striving to place a mental icon of Alyson in the fore of his mind, but that didn't work. He tried Ken, but that failed, too.

Desperate, he had recourse to an image he had resurrected when, at Quentin's age, he was forever given to instant arousal. He invoked the ludicrous vision of Baron von Munchausen's legendary horse, cut in half and drinking at a trough, a stream of water flowing perpetually from the back part of the severed trunk. That he hoped frantically would halt the growing arousal of his member even if he couldn't prevent what he knew was its initial stirring. "We must get back," he muttered weakly. "The others will be waiting."

Suddenly, for no comprehensible motive, at least from nothing he had done save in the secrecy of his rebellious erotic thoughts, Quentin kissed Davey on the cheek. "Poor Uncle Davey," he said. "It's so hard for you, isn't it? I wish I hadn't only brought Nigel. I wish I'd brought my boyfriend, Gavin, too."

Davey began to cry. By the time his tears were gone, Quentin had become the comforter, the surrogate for Ken. There in the silver mine's tower, hidden from the world, their roles were reversed. Hugged to young Quentin's willing breast, the older man became the child.

When Davey's sobs subsided, the two moved apart, each seeking words to heal the rawness of revelation, to control the legacy of unbidden emotions. Quentin was the first to speak. "I don't think we should mention anything about this. Let's just say it was something between us, between two Bryant generations up here on your moor."

Davey looked down toward the murk of the hard ground. He closed his eyes, but it was his thoughts he wanted to shut off. "Of course," he said mechanically. "It would serve no good purpose to tell." Quickly he broadened the implication of his words. "It's up to you when you tell anyone about anything. Coming out I mean to someone like your mother and Hester. No one can do that for you. Ken and I are absolutely united on that."

Quentin was already scrambling back toward the daylight. "Give me your hand," he suggested, "and I'll give you a yank up." This time the whole process was without a trace of self-consciousness.

Davey never did tell his young relative about Aunt Nora's confessions.

TWENTY-ONE

Alyson lay between the two men as her children pranced about the vast, clean carpet of sand the tide revealed in its retreat. Temporary pools gleamed in the sun, and the two tiny islands of Greenaway and Gull Rock, remote in the bay, looked calm and inviting. Pentire Head afforded needed shade for those aging skins whose anxious owners had been instructed by their physicians to shelter from the sun's still vigorous rays.

She sighed with satisfaction at a perfect October afternoon in her native county. It wasn't hard to see her son and daughter as younger than they were. Then, as her cousin had just observed as he also watched them closely, there was nothing like a beach to shed the years for everyone—to turn discontented teenagers into carefree children, to remind the middle-aged with their new waistlines of what they had recently left behind.

It was also able to stir such as he and Ken to a gentle nostalgia for those countless seaside summers, from infant bucket-and-spade days to daring sex in the dunes, and latterly, contented lizardlike immobility on the sun-warmed rocks along the Sunshine Coast of British Columbia.

Lying stretched out there now on that season-emptied beach filled each of them in diverse ways with their long pasts: Ken of his Laguna days in prewar California, not least that December 7 when play-intent children and somnolent sun worshippers were rudely reminded of Pearl Harbor and the arrival of war; Davey on that very beach of Polzeath when he brimmed with pubescent excitement at the sight of beautiful white-furred seal cubs barking as orphans in deep, dark caves, and a little later—and a lot less innocently—steering his surfboard through the spume as he imagined he was Esther Williams, Hollywood's Queen of the Surf.

For Alyson beaches weren't normally a passport to blissful memories. On the Falmouth ones in whose neighbourhood she had spent most of her childhood—the family home having bordered one—an overzealous mother had made certain that beaches were no invitation to freedom or a place where life could be seen from a different perspective. There were German submarines, relics from World War I, stranded under low cliffs at the head of some beaches, but such were strictly forbidden for a little girl, an only child of mutually jealous and ever-warring parents.

She had to be content to watch liberated boys leap from a submarine's small and rusting deck down to the beach, and others clambering up the fascinating conning towers of the berthed vessels from a long-dead war and a faraway country. The relatively calm sea at the mouth of the English Channel was considered impossibly dangerous for her to bathe in, al fresco picnics were impossibly vulgar, and destinations that encouraged "trippers" in summertime, were certainly not the places where refined Falmouth daughters should be seen. Considering the Bryants' proximity to all these things, Alyson was forced to spend most of her summer days in the confines of her garden, which was screened from the vulgar gaze by a line of imported Canary Islands palms interspersed with thick clumps of marram grass, thus procuring the desired sense of both great expense and intimidating privacy.

The exception to this prison routine, of course, was the annual visits to Davey's parents. Then, for two glorious weeks, everything seemed halcyon. First, she had the delight of her slightly older cousin to afford her a sense of the two of them being shared children in a family, an antidote, however brief, from the incessant loneliness that assailed her at home. And Davey's parents—in conjunction sometimes with Uncle Joseph and Aunt Hannah—made a welcome relief from her implacably Puritan mother and a father whose vocabulary, at least as far as it applied to his only child, was the one word *no*.

Thankfully Uncle Wesley and Aunt Constance—in the brief time she was alive during the earlier of these holiday visits—acted as if children were actually welcome on the planet and had pursuits and pleasures that were legitimately theirs. One such delight was the series of casual pasty picnics on this particular beach of Polzeath with its miles of sand, exciting surf, and mysterious caves with dripping tongue ferns at their entrance and deep, dark pools full of darting blenny with their blunt heads and bulging eyes.

Before the swimming in warm pools or in the happy-sounding sea were the generously jam-and-clotted-cream-smeared yeast buns after the pasties themselves and washed down with lemonade or ginger beer, all food and drink that would have prohibited not only swimming but any physical exercise until taking an enforced nap back home amid the restrictions of Falmouth.

Alyson remembered as she propped herself against a convenient rock and wriggled plump toes in the cool, silvery sand that those days, ludicrously brief though they were, had given her a taste of heaven she had sworn even then she would strive to pass on if she were ever to become a mother with a little girl. Well, she had ended up with a little boy, too.

She started guiltily. Two boys, in fact. She thought of Allen away in St. Bride's and felt a traitor at her pleasurable sense of freedom from all restriction, just as she had when a girl. To escape the thrall she turned to Davey. "Lying here like this I wonder why Mother and Father seemed to completely forget what was supposed to be good for me at home and allowed me to live like you and your family did for those two weeks."

He smiled at her. "I think Auntie Muriel was so busy fighting with Daddy over religion and everything and your dad was so lost in his sense of superior wealth that you were forgotten for the time being. Their pleasure was a fortnight's slumming with the relatives, and your mum proving how superior her Methodism was over everybody else's beliefs. They hardly had an extra moment to think about you."

Alyson nodded, fully in agreement. "That's why, Davey, I'm determined my kids don't ever have to go through all that. Whatever they do or believe, they'll never see me acting as their judge or jailer."

This time Davey didn't respond. He returned his sight to Quentin, a slim silhouette against the ribbon of retreating waves. Davey wondered what she would make of things should her son ever tell her he was gay. He had heard only too often of mothers of kids who had come out to them, suddenly full of misgivings and guilt at not observing or guiding their offspring more closely in their growing up. Davey closed his eyes. He had made a pact with Quentin. Besides, he was now determined not to make it his business.

Ken flicked a casual glance at the pile of clothes and diving equipment the youngsters had quickly abandoned when the expanse of sea, sand, and air had beckoned. Satisfied that everything was in its place, smiling inwardly at himself for even vaguely worrying as there was no one anywhere near them on the beach, he returned to what he had previously been ruminating.

It wasn't Quentin who had been preoccupying him but the boy's sister. That same morning, seizing a hasty moment while traversing Lanoe when the two of them found themselves parted from her mother, Hester had suddenly approached him and blurted what amounted to a scrambled confession into his startled ear. She told him she now had a boyfriend. That his name was Tim. That he also lived in Notting Hill, and that he was black, though the term she used was *West Indian*. She also implied they were sleeping together whenever they could.

It wasn't all this, though, that prompted his present reflection, or the fact that he'd thought about little else since they had all reassembled and embarked on this afternoon outing. Just before her mother's heavy approach up the creaking stairs had heralded her arrival, Hester had grabbed his arm and stammeringly offered her bombshell. "Oh, and by the way, Uncle Ken, I was due for my period this week and nothing's happened. It always occurs pretty regularly, but I don't take the pill or anything. And I don't know anything about abortions."

The door of Hannah's sitting room wasn't shut. Within seconds Ken expected to see Alyson's ample frame fill the space. "I'll get back to you," he whispered. "Don't do anything. Don't tell anyone. Not till we can talk. I'll try tonight."

And that was where it had ended: ragged and raw, her swallowing what he could see were incipient tears as her mother entered the room and asked, jokingly, if they'd found any more secrets about poor Hannah and Nora and their unhappy dog.

Ken was still pondering this turn of events when the youngsters returned and suggested they trek to the rocks below Pentire where snorkelling, Quentin had read in a travel magazine, was most popular.

All three adults seemed only too keen to get up and move, and it wasn't long before they were reinstalled in positions where they could observe from a low-lying stretch of sea-burned turf on which they laid towels both Hester diving impetuously from the steepest rocks and Quentin, alternatively, mainly submerged and presumably peering at underwater sights with the aid of his snorkel.

Alyson was sitting up as she peered down at the heaving sea that frothed against a few rocks that broke the surface. By coming out along the headland, they had long passed where the waves broke upon Polzeath Beach. Where they were now the ocean was quite deep and at a point where the receding tide never reached. She suddenly reached over to her cousin and asked him if he would descend a little lower and see if he could make out her son swimming underwater.

Davey nodded quickly and sprang up to do as he was bid. Overhead a buzzard mewed as it circled in the azure, and he tried to recall if any superstitions had been attached to the blunt-winged birds by his father. He remembered being told of the illness brought by the raven's croak, the magpie that needed the doffing of your hat to turn away anger, the holy power of the robin, and the wickedness of the wren. But mercifully, nothing he could think of embraced buzzards!

He climbed carefully down the slatey slope until he could see the spread-eagled form of his young cousin as a dark shape above the sand. It took a few moments before he realized the boy wasn't moving. He looked up anxiously toward Alyson, but she was out of sight. Instead he caught the glance of Hester who was about to dive again but wore a look of triumph on her young face.

That meant nothing to him as rising panic rose in his chest. "Check out Quentin!" he screamed above the crashing waves. "I think he's stuck or something." Even as he shouted he was tearing off his shirt. Just as he threw his septuagenarian body into the grey-green swell, he saw that she had already dived. When his head bobbed back to the surface and he looked toward where he prayed he'd last seen Quentin, he glimpsed her rise like a slim young seal from the water, the dark gold tousled head of her brother in her outstretched arms as she backstroked vigorously in the direction of the water's edge. In seconds he was at her side, and then, in swimming unison, they towed Quentin as they swam toward a tiny cove, invisible from above and which was carpeted with stark white pebbles. It was on their smoothness that they laid his limp body. Together they applied violent massage and together they slumped with relief when the body under their fingers stiffened, water slid out of his mouth, and Quentin opened his blue eyes.

There were gulls down there closer to the sea, and it was above their cries that Davey heard the wail of his cousin. He nudged Hester. "Get up there to her. I'll manage with him. Quentin?"

The boy nodded, smiled, and glanced at the older man. "Thank you for rescuing me."

Davey turned to the boy's sister to apologize for the mistake, but she was already scrambling up the cliff face, the pale moons of her bottom growing smaller by the second.

"It was your sister who saved you, Quentin. I was just the backup."

The youth nodded, but the eventful day was not to finish before Davey learned that such was not the interpretation the young man chose to put on the overall incident.

On the cliff top, when all were reunited, there was laughter and jokes but no signs of hysterical relief. It was only then that Davey realized Hester hadn't presented her mother and Ken with a dramatic picture. In fact, the salient details of the rescue of Quentin from certain drowning were deliberately held from his doting mother for a very long time.

TWENTY-TWO

Jack Pascoe was nothing if not a true Celtic colonial. Once he accepted that Canadian Davey, his English cousin Alyson Bolitho, plus their recently arrived cohorts were disposed to be free with their money, all the previous irritants—such as the patronizing attitudes and attempts to identify with the Cornish locals—were instantly banished and the causes, likes, and dislikes of the out-of-season residents of the Cornish Arms were loudly trumpeted by the turncoat landlord, indeed asserted as having Gospel authority! His new attitude was given special emphasis after receiving a visit from the distaff member of the newly minted Frocins of Tintagel.

Hilda Verran wasn't in a mood to hedge matters. Craning her neck to see her quarry busy behind the bar, she launched her diminutive self in his direction, skillfully avoiding the outstretched legs and feet of late-morning customers and lifting the hem of her startlingly bright saffron dress wherever she saw beer puddles. Hilda was wearing the stupid gown, which attracted the attention of most of the bar as they had never before seen either that hue or the length of the garment in their moorland village, to appease her husband.

Len hadn't been keen to be left alone, bereft of her verbal armour, while they were still shooting sequences along the narrow streets of Tintagel and erstwhile neighbours and acquaintances were prone to shout rude retorts at the little man in his newly flagrant colours. Hilda, however, had been adamant. It was one thing to see Lanoe pass from under their spited noses—in contrast to Hannah's expressed verbal desire or not—simply because he was disposed to impress a bunch of foreigners, but they owned Kelly Green cottage, which stood adjacent to Lanoe and was unhappily empty.

If there was one thing that could drive her to a frenzy, it was owning property that wasn't paying for itself, as she put it, and when Len allowed he wasn't interested in spending much time with the mean-minded peasantry of Pentudy now that the new life of the screen had opened up before him, she was determined to do something about the crumbling, cobwalled cottage with its sagging, lichened slate roof that she insisted was picturesque.

As so often with the two of them, life ran on a quid pro quo basis, which was the reason she'd reluctantly surrendered to Len's wishes and was wearing the miniature gown meant to evoke the Arthurian Middle Ages as she headed for Jack Pascoe who had once expressed the thought he might be interested in buying Kelly Green from them.

Freeing herself from the clinging folds of the skirt, she managed to clamber up the one unoccupied bar stool where she could more or less confront the landlord face-to-face. "Oi didn' phone beforehand, maister, as we was busy wi'd all that BBC filmin', but Oi come to maike on 'ee an offer Oi do believe you dursn' refuse."

Pascoe paused, full pint tankard of cider in hand. Old Fred Nankivell could wait a second or so if the dwarf had come to talk money. "How's that then, missus?" He decided to play up to the bar. "Come to offer some of us playin' parts, is that it? They BBC buggers did up and away fast enough from Pentudy. Oi do reckon 'twere only the loikes on you they wanted here. Save a few snaps of the moor, that is."

Fred Nankivell decided he was thirsty for another pint. He pushed his pensioner's legs up from where he sat with his silver-haired cronies and crawled crablike to the bar. He smiled at the landlord. "If that be for me what you'm holdin' in your hand, then Oi'll be payin' for it and taike me leave, maister, while you drummin' up trade for the village."

Pascoe returned a smile as empty as the one he'd received and plunked the tankard down before the crusty customer. The landlord could have sworn the old man deliberately gave him the smallest coins possible as he slowly dropped each of them into the publican's open palm.

It was Hilda's turn to insist on attention. "Course, if you'm too busy, Oi can try elsewhere. 'Tis only that you, yourself, mentioned it once and 'tis what we in the business do call a very desirable property! We be lettin' of her go for a song, you."

She had his attention totally then and mentioned a price he knew was cheap and which he'd have loved to have agreed to then and there. The trouble was Pascoe at that moment wasn't feeling all that fiscally flush. He was experiencing no financial problems per se; it was only that while he was comfortable on a day-to-day basis, there was nothing over for a substantial outlay of the kind she was suggesting. He bit his lower lip, then turned the tip of his tongue up to trace the length of his razor-thin moustache. It was then he had his brainwave. His features relaxed and he proffered her the closest to a sincere smile he could manage. "Oi got an idea, missus. There's people Oi do know who might well be interested."

Hilda was disappointed. "Well, that price can't stay forever, you. Once it do get out."

He felt close to panic. "Oi'll talk to 'em this afternoon. Oi'll give 'ee an answer by this evenin'. Oi can tell 'ee roight now 'tis as good as done. Oi do know they be lookin' for a desirable residence in the village, and Kelly Green would be roight up their alley!"

He took her rather soiled business card with the Verrans' phone number. Len had scrawled "Dwarfs of Tintagel" on it, but she forbear comment and so did its recipient. Pascoe could hardly get rid of her fast enough as he contemplated bringing his proposal up with Davey and his lawyer friend and suggest that a comfortable cottage next to Lanoe would provide an excellent spillover for guests in the future. In his mind he had already doubled the figure she'd mentioned.

What he had now dubbed the "Canadian Party" arrived home in the early evening, and the landlord could tell at once they were in good spirits and thus, he felt, in excellent mood to hear his proposition and hopefully to act upon it.

TWENTY-THREE

D avey and his retinue were hardly inside the inn when Jack Pascoe pounced. "Welcome home, the Lanoe Family! Had a bravun good toime at Polzeath, Oi do hope?"

They replied affirmatively and in unison.

The landlord selected his target, choosing Alyson. "May Oi have a word with 'ee, missus? Sorry to butt in and that, but this is something that do require a bit of haste." He manoeuvred her toward the end of the bar. The room was empty, as it was still seconds before opening time. "Oi jest heard the property next to your'n be empty and is goin' for a song." He caught the blank look and cursed his choice. The stupid cow didn't even know he was referring to Lanoe House! He soon had extra reason to regret choosing Alyson.

"I think you'd better talk to Mr. Bradley or my cousin, Mr. Pascoe. Ken is a lawyer and is used to handling things like that. And anything he and Davey decide is all right by me."

But the publican was already seeking Ken's attention, raising his voice to do so. Ken detached himself from the youngsters, approaching with a smile and raised eyebrows. This time Pascoe didn't waste words in preamble. "The empty cottage next to Lanoe is goin' for a pretty song. Oi been instructed to let it go for two thousand poun', the owners not being here to Pentudy and wantin' to get rid of the plaice so soon as they can. Oi immediately thought of you folks, squire. Kelly Green, you see, wouldn' only give on 'ee spillover room for extra guests when you all be here but will see you allus got privacy to the north and up to the moor if 'ee did taike of 'un. 'Cos 'tis worth at least double that and will be snapped up if 'ee don' grab of 'un."

Ken ignored the latter. Instead he smiled evenly at the anxious landlord. "And what's the catch then? There usually is one if the price is especially low."

"Fuckin' lawyers!" went unspoken through Pascoe's mind. "On the contrary, maister, 'tis all fair and open. Why don' all on 'ee come over and have a look-see for yourself? Key's over there under the mantel. 'Tis a bravun pretty property if you asks Oi."

"Give me a moment with the gang," Ken said, signalling to his party to go out to the corridor. Out there, with Alyson and Davey behind him, he relayed what Pascoe had told him. He then reminded the four of them that they had Lanoe House without any payment save minor legal fees and, after what they had seen that morning, the cost of a few repairs to make the place habitable. He was inclined to make the whole business contingent upon the state in which they found the cottage he thought they should most certainly inspect.

The upshot of this was to extract an agreement that they immediately go and take a look at Kelly Green and then inform the landlord of the Cornish Arms sometime that evening what decision they had arrived at. Davey, however, said he would leave it in the hands of the others. At the last moment, and slightly to Davey's consternation, Quentin announced he, too, would stay at the pub and keep his "uncle" company.

In the event that was precisely what happened, with Pascoe

returning to his duties as landlord shortly thereafter. He found Davey and Quentin in the visitors' lounge where he jovially informed them he had told Ken where to replace the great iron key when the inspection of the cottage was concluded. The man was obviously pleased by their initial reactions.

The whole operation resulted in dinner, which would be served to them in private in that very same room, being shifted back to somewhat later than what they were accustomed to. There were other implications to the change of schedule, as well. By the time Ken had been dispatched to say the Bryant family was interested in concluding a deal over the small cottage, they were informed that dinner would be some forty minutes away. Davey and Quentin had both drunk half pints of ale during the absence of the others and now, in consort with the rest, decided to switch to gin and tonics as a prelude to what they all now dubbed the Farewell Supper.

The result of all this as the mealtime hove closer was not that anyone was drunk but that all were distinctly more lively than when they had originally gotten back from Polzeath. Not so much in raised voices, though such did occur, but in a bolder body language was this change demonstrated.

Hester, for instance, after excitedly whispering to Ken that her violent diving bouts had indeed affected her in that her period had returned soon after her return to dry land, now insisted on clambering onto his lap until her mother, smile vanishing, firmly told her to return to her seat. Quentin, slightly less ambitious, had clasped Davey's hand across the table where they sat with their glasses, and insisted on murmuring gentle nothings about his prowess as swimmer and saviour. Alyson forced herself not to linger or reflect on her son's odd behaviour. Instead she returned to her preferred stance of slumping her weight and smiling, this time at Ken, who in turn beamed back.

"I think that old Kelly Green might be a great investment," he told her. "Of course, it could do with running water instead of that pump in the kitchen, and I think you'd want to get rid of the oil lamps and have electricity installed. It occurs to me that we might save some expense by having that run direct from Lanoe, which I notice has its own wind-powered generator."

"You say 'we' Ken, but it's up to us and not you fellows to pay for the likes of that. That is if the children and I decide we want to use the place regularly to get out of London for a space. It's up to them, of course."

"On the contrary," Ken argued. "We would very likely use it, too." He looked quickly at his lover. "That is if Davey is so willing."

All Davey knew at that moment, even though his heart was warm with a little gin and his thoughts softly muzzy from the same source, was that memory-soaked Lanoe wasn't a place he particularly wished to visit in the immediate future.

Then Quentin squeezed Davey's hand again. "Each time you guys come over Davey has promised to show me more of his moors. I'm looking forward to you doing that a lot. I didn't know how much I was missing in the past!"

Alyson looked benign, at once forgiving her impetuous son's outstretched arm. "That's very nice, Quentin. And when we get the cottage fixed up you can have your little friends down to stay, as well. Those school friends you're always talking about."

And those he *never* talks about, Davey thought. He shuddered wickedly at his naughty glimpse of the future. "I think it will be so different when we all get together here. It certainly won't be the same for me with those horrible Frocins no longer plaguing me, and by then I hope the ghosts of poor Hannah and Nora and all their problems will be well and truly laid." He looked fondly at the boy across from him. "And, of course, there are the moors," he added softly, intending his words for those particular ears.

Almost coincidentally with that, Jack Pascoe himself arrived, bearing a huge tureen of soup which, when its steel lid was removed, revealed a steaming concoction of parsnips and leeks.

They all at once crossed to the laid table where the meal was to be eaten, but in their seating Hester sat next to Ken and Quentin next to Davey. Alyson sat as queen mother between the two men from Canada.

The new grouping appeared to sexually savvy Pascoe on his frequent appearances during the lengthy meal as if it had always been thus. He would have been doubtless surprised if, after the repast was completed and a truly satiated quintet sat back on scattered chairs and sofas, that the social dynamics reverted to a past era. Davey and Ken shared a chintz sofa with a sleepy Alyson, while the children, chattering together, sat on two armchairs.

TWENTY-FOUR

Back on the Sunshine Coast in British Columbia, Davey and Ken trudged through the nearby arbutus grove toward the cliffs where belted kingfishers hurled their black-and-white bodies toward the grey surface of the Pacific far below. The walk was Davey's idea, but Ken had readily concurred. The two days since their return hadn't been easy for him. Davey had nightly called Alyson in London and had used both occasions to talk also to Quentin.

That didn't bother the retired lawyer very much, but he did note that Davey never mentioned the boy when giving a résumé of his conversations with his sister. On the other hand, when Hester interrupted her mother and asked to talk to Ken—to ratify her menstrual health and repeat her relief in having so miraculously escaped pregnancy—he didn't feel it incumbent to relate all *that* to his partner. It was his tit-for-tat. In any case, he argued to himself, it was privileged information that professionally he couldn't divulge. At a more human level he also derived a pleasantly avuncular feeling from knowing the young girl had implicit trust in his discretion.

But this novel element of less than total candour between them wasn't the only discordant factor in the household. Equally significant, in Ken's anxious eyes, was his lover's inability to shed the sense of anxiety and even rootlessness he had brought back with him. Davey would wander from room to room, touching objects but not responding to them, glancing out windows but with no registry in his eyes. Or again Ken would call him to help in some small chore—moving the extra leaf from the dining-room table, emptying the dishwasher—but received no reaction whatsoever. At least not for an exceptionally long space of time. Only after that would his companion drag himself off the leather sofa in the window bay, where he invariably draped himself, to perform reluctantly whatever task Ken had suggested.

Nor did his sense of Davey's disquiet end there. In bed his partner would lie on his back and tell Ken in disjointed spurts of words how disillusioned the Cornwall visit had made him, how cut off he now felt from so much he had hitherto taken for granted. "I can now think of myself as one of those poor postwar bastards they used to call DPs, those no longer with a country or even a sense of identity."

At different moments in those late-night hours Davey would laugh aloud, waking his companion up, as in a harsh voice he'd say, "You know what, Ken? I think I now know what it must feel like to be a raped girl, a maiden who's just lost her virginity!"

The first night back Ken had cuddled him as tears had finally welled. The second night Davey lay in bed, his mouth stubbornly closed, his staring eyes facing the curtain-billowing window and the stars. But Ken knew his lover continued to lie there for more hours before sleep eventually took him.

This was now the third day. As if sensing the portentousness of that, the couple had almost grabbed their outdoors clothes and scampered rather than walked their way to the site Davey had chosen and over which his partner had so willingly acquiesced.

What he was expecting, the transplanted Cornishman wasn't quite sure. It wasn't the view, since from the cliff top looking west there wasn't really one. Just to their north was Texada Island and immediately opposite, though usually no more than a smudge or a faint silhouette, were the niveous mountaintops of Vancouver Island. On the seashores of British Columbia there was sometimes the excitement of killer whales cruising in pod formation the lengths of the creeks, or rhythmically appearing and disappearing amid the chop of the open sea. And if they were lucky, standing there, silent in introspection, waiting for nature to nudge, otters might appear in the kelp, while eagles circled majestically overhead.

On this day all these things happened. Davey thought it was to do with the fact that in the woodlands he had glimpsed the white scut of a deer. He liked to think it was the same one he'd seen before journeying to Hannah's funeral. In any case, he'd made a wish that there would be things to see. He wasn't sure if spotting the same deer twice was a specifically Cornish lucky omen, but he told himself it must surely be a local Indian one.

That got him thinking, and when they finally stood in the sturdy breeze, not dissimilar from the one he had left behind on the Cornish coast, he began to open up to a waiting Ken. "I suppose you could call the Cornish the equivalents over there of the Coastal Salish and the others. The English have fucked up their place just like what's happened here."

Ken smiled. His inclination was to warn about being too simplistic, but his instinct told him his lover wouldn't appreciate such a caution. "Well, I'd never thought of it that way. But I guess if you're a First Nations type and knew about your previous life as a hunter and fisherman and now lived around somewhere like today's Vancouver you could be pretty pissed off by what's happened."

Davey mulled over that. "Salmon's disappearing. Sturgeon's harder and harder to find in the Fraser River. Local abalone's gone. Those huge geoduck clams, they're on the way out, aren't they?

Not to mention our forests, the few remaining groves of Garry oak. And that's just a handful of disasters, and for every one of them I can give you a Cornish equivalent. With the total death of the Cornish language thrown in to boot! And who doesn't think that the Native languages aren't on their way out around here?"

Ken was wondering where all this was taking his friend. "So?"

Davey suddenly grinned. "So I haven't come very far, have I? Just exchanged one situation with another very similar."

"Only you're not an Indian."

"Nor am I some kind of Cornish Brit. I'm a Canadian citizen, for Christ's sake! In any case, I'm not talking passports or nationalities. It's just that everything that shaped me has been cancelled out. It isn't a matter of legal technicalities. Those things simply don't matter. It's just that my heritage has been obliterated. No big deal really." He tried to make it sound wry rather than bitter.

Ken was very silent, sensing treacherous ground between them. But then the sun came out from the overhead canopy of high cloud. Or for the ex-Californian the human equivalent happened. His lover suddenly raised his arms, like a bishop uplifting them in blessing. "As the Indians say, you don't have to own it like whitey, having the documents, the deeds, that is, but all this is ours. *Spiritually* ours. And we can do our bloody best to see it doesn't become another Cornwall. Not just for them, the earlier settlers, but for all of us. We all sink if we let the whole place simply go commercial, become like parts of what I've just experienced."

Ken hugged him, though it was more relief than romantic ardour. "You're dead-on, mate," he said, using their family favourite mock Aussie. "Balance is what it's all about, cobber, but balance isn't the stuff poetry is made of. It's just something you have to keep bloody working for, whatever it bloody takes, wherever you bloody are."

He reverted to his normal English. "Don't forget, Davey, you still have a stake over there. You, Alyson, and the kids, you've still got Lanoe—and now with Kelly Green thrown in." He paused. "I guess what I'm saying is that we can do something about at least keeping Pentudy unspoiled, as well as your precious moors."

"You're beginning to sound like a politician. Next you'll be standing for the Green Party!"

Ken punched him playfully. "I just want my old Davey. I'd stand as a whorehouse madam if that 'ud do the trick."

Davey neatly turned the talk. "Quentin is gay."

Ken paused while thinking. Then he winked. "Hester isn't pregnant."

They both began to laugh with such mutual abandon that it was as if they had personally invented the emotion.

AUTHOR'S STATEMENT

Although a culmination of the series begun back in 1978 with *No More into the Garden* and involving my protagonists, Davey Bryant (in this particular fiction a retired newspaper editor) and Ken Bradley (now a retired lawyer), I did not conceive this book as any kind of swan song. The fact that the two men return to the metaphorical garden indicates, not a change of heart, but a defiance of the writer's original intention! Through several novels and story collections they have travelled much, visited many places and, hopefully, learned to love each other more deeply. But not to be fully reconciled to settling down. Perhaps a special problem, given the facility of transportation, for today's emigrant/immigrant anywhere?

Authorial instinct told me that something more had to happen; something of certain spiritual and psychological magnitude to do with a twentieth-century transplant putting down fresh roots that could only be truly effected by drastic readjustment and unqualified reconciliation. And for this daunting task Davey must have not only self-knowledge but the guidance and strength that is the benison of unstinted and unqualified love from the faithful Ken.

To implement all this, Davey, now the elderly Canadian immigrant, still required the severing of a final obstructive tug of *Heimweh*, a homesickness demanding a last return to his birthplace to achieve a full and final reconciliation with his ongoing West Coast Canadian life shared with the ex-Californian Ken at the dawn of a new century.

In that respect, then, this novel addresses unfinished business. I cannot bury my character, who made his debut in my short-story collection *Ashes for Easter* in 1972, but at least I can now let him go to live if not at rest, then in peace. Yet, as in life itself, one situation leads swiftly to an undreamed other. In this Cornish case the new challenge proved to be one where ancient myths still swirl, dark secrets are revealed, and the Celtic claims of family refuse to be silenced. In other words, the matter of a novel whose specific substance I knew nothing about until it was written.

MORE NEW FICTION FROM BEACH HOLME

Cold Clear Morning
by Lesley Choyce
NOVEL $18.95 CDN $14.95 US ISBN: 0-88878-416-3

Taylor Colby and his childhood sweetheart, Laura, abandoned their Nova Scotia coastal village home for a life in the high-octane world of rock music in California. Now, after Laura's drug-related death, Taylor has returned to his roots to live once again with his noble but isolated boatbuilder father. Complicating matters further, Taylor's mother, who has been battling cancer, attempts to reconcile with both her husband and son whom she deserted decades earlier.

Hail Mary Corner
by Brian Payton
NOVEL $18.95 CDN ISBN: 0-88878-422-8

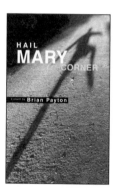

High on a cliff overlooking a pulp-mill town in British Columbia, sixteen-year-old Bill MacAvoy and his friends lead cloistered lives when other boys their age run free. It may be the fall of 1982, but inside the walls of their Benedictine seminary they inhabit a medieval society steeped in ritual and discipline—a world where black-robed monks move like shadows between doubt and faith.

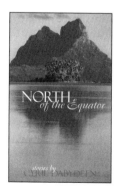

North of the Equator
by Cyril Dabydeen
SHORT FICTION $18.95 CDN $14.95 US ISBN: 0-88878-423-6

Cyril Dabydeen's new collection of stories, *North of the Equator*, looks at the polarities of tropical and temperate places. Acclaimed novelist Sam Selvon (*The Lonely Londoners*) says, "Dabydeen is in the vanguard of contemporary short-story writers, shuttling with equal and consummate skill from rural Guyana to metropolitan Canada." Dabydeen's characters live in limbo, stretched between two worlds: one, an adopted home in Canada; the other, a birthplace in the islands scattered across the equator.

BEACH HOLME PUBLISHING • WWW.BEACHHOLME.BC.CA